Am

Elise stared at Matt for a long moment, her heart pulsing.

What would he do if she kissed him? Just reached up on tiptoe and pulled his head down to hers? The moment stretched out between them, as bright and hopeful as those fairy lights dripping from the eaves of the nearby house. She drew up on her toes inside her boots…then chickened out and slid back down to the ground.

Her gaze flashed to his again and her stomach trembled at the intensity in his eyes and a moment later, his mouth brushed hers.

His lips were warm and firm and he tasted of chocolate and mint.

She closed her eyes and leaned into his strength. The night seemed magical. She felt so safe here, warm and content, a slow peace soaking through her.

She swallowed her impulse of earlier and rose up on her toes so she could wrap her arms around his neck, savoring the heat of him.

She was in deep trouble.

Dear Reader,

I love stories about secret crushes that unexpectedly turn into something more, especially if that shift happens when a woman is least expecting it…and when she most needs something solid to hold on to.

Elise Clifton has always had a bit of a thing for (mostly) reformed troublemaker Matt Cates—but right now, she's not looking for love.

The foundation of her world has been shaken after the discovery that her entire identity had been based on a mistake. Hurting and alone during the holidays, she desperately needs a strong shoulder and turns to her old friend Matt. Much to her shock, Matt wants much more from Elise.

I had a truly magical time writing their story, giving Elise and Matt the happy ending they deserve and coming to know all the Thunder Canyon Cowboys!

All the best of the season to you and your loved ones.

RaeAnne Thayne

A THUNDER CANYON CHRISTMAS

RAEANNE THAYNE

Silhouette®

SPECIAL EDITION®

Published by Silhouette Books

America's Publisher of Contemporary Romance

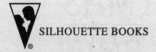

SILHOUETTE BOOKS

ISBN-13: 978-0-373-65565-6

A THUNDER CANYON CHRISTMAS

Recycling programs
for this product may
not exist in your area.

Books by RaeAnne Thayne

Silhouette Special Edition

††*Light the Stars* #1748
††*Dancing in the Moonlight* #1757
††*Dalton's Undoing* #1764
***The Daddy Makeover* #1857
***His Second-Chance Family* #1874
§*A Merger...or Marriage?* #1903
***A Soldier's Secret* #1918
††*The Cowboy's Christmas Miracle* #1933
‡*Fortune's Woman* #1970
††*A Cold Creek Homecoming* #1996
††*A Cold Creek Holiday* #2013
††*A Cold Creek Secret* #2025
††*A Cold Creek Baby* #2071
‡‡*A Thunder Canyon Christmas* #2083

*Outlaw Hartes
†The Searchers
††The Cowboys of Cold Creek
**The Women of Brambleberry House
§The Wilder Family
‡Fortunes of Texas: Return to Red Rock
‡‡Montana Mavericks: Thunder Canyon Cowboys

Silhouette Romantic Suspense

The Wrangler and the Runaway Mom #960
Saving Grace #995
Renegade Father #1062
**The Valentine Two-Step* #1133
**Taming Jesse James* #1139
**Cassidy Harte and the Comeback Kid* #1144
The Quiet Storm #1218
Freefall #1239
Nowhere to Hide #1264
†*Nothing to Lose* #1321
†*Never Too Late* #1364
The Interpreter #1380
High-Risk Affair #1448
Shelter from the Storm #1467
High-Stakes Honeymoon #1475

RAEANNE THAYNE

finds inspiration in the beautiful northern Utah mountains, where she lives with her husband and three children. Her books have won numerous honors, including three RITA® Award nominations from Romance Writers of America and a Career Achievement Award from *RT Book Reviews* magazine. RaeAnne loves to hear from readers and can be reached through her website at www.raeannethayne.com.

Chapter One

Rock bottom was one thing. This had to be a new low, even for her.

Elise Clifton hunched onto the bar stool at The Hitching Post, painfully aware of her solitary status. She wasn't sure which made her more pathetic—showing up alone at Thunder Canyon's favorite watering hole or the fact that she would rather be anywhere else on earth, including here by herself, than home with her family right now.

She sipped at her drink, trying to avoid meeting anyone's gaze.

So much for the girls' night out she had been eagerly anticipating all week. She was supposed to have met her best friend Haley Anderson here for a night of margaritas and girl talk, accompanied by a popular local band.

Two out of three was still a winning average, she supposed.

The band was here, a trio of cute, edgy long-haired cowboys belting out crowd-pleasing rockabilly music. Margaritas, check. She was almost done with her second and heading fast toward number three.

But the girl talk was notably lacking...maybe because Haley had called her twenty minutes ago, her voice hoarse and full of apologies.

"I'm so sorry I didn't phone you earlier," Haley had rasped out. "I completely zonked and slept through my alarm. All day I've been hoping the cold medicine would finally kick in and I would be ready to rock and roll with you at The Hitching Post. No luck, though. It's only making me so sleepy I'm not consciously aware of how miserable I feel."

"Don't worry about it," Elise had answered, trying to keep any trace of her plummeting mood out of her voice. She couldn't really blame Haley for her bad luck in coming down with a lousy cold on a night when Elise was particularly desperate for any available diversion. She would be a poor friend to make a big deal about it, especially when Haley probably felt even worse than she sounded, which was pretty bad.

"We can reschedule as soon as you're feeling better," Elise had said. "The Hitching Post will still be here in a week or two."

"Deal," Haley croaked out. "If I ever get feeling better, anyway. Right now that doesn't seem likely."

"You will. Hang in there."

That was about the time Elise had gestured for her second margarita as her plans for the evening went up in smoke.

"Thanks for understanding, honey. First round is on me next time."

Elise sighed now as the band switched songs to one she hadn't heard before. She watched the blinking of Christmas lights that some enterprising soul had draped around the racy picture of Lily Divine adorned in strategically placed gauze that hung above the bar.

Even Lily Divine was in a holiday mood. Too bad Elise couldn't say the same.

Usually she enjoyed coming to The Hitching Post. Once rumored to be Thunder Canyon's house of ill repute, the place was now a warm, welcoming bar and grill. Locals loved it for its enduring nature. Unlike the rest of Thunder Canyon, The Hitching Post had remained unchanged through the ebbs and flows of the local economy.

With hardwood floors, the same weathered old bar and framed photos from the 1880s on the walls, the restaurant and bar likely hadn't changed much since the days when Lily Divine herself used to preside over the saloon she'd inherited from the original madam.

Elise had never been here by herself, though, and was quickly discovering how that created an entirely different dynamic. She felt more alone than ever as she sipped her drink and tried to avoid making eye contact. With a lone woman in a bar like The Hitching Post, it probably looked as if she was on the prowl, in search of some big, strong cowboy to help her while away a cold winter's night.

One such cowboy—a little heavy on the outdoorsy aftershave—sat three stools away. He'd been eyeing her for the past ten minutes and she was trying her best to pretend she didn't notice.

Maybe if she had stayed at Clifton's Pride, she might have been snuggled up right now in a fleece blanket watching some movie on the big-screen television at her family's ranch house instead of perched here at the bar like some kind of sad, pathetic loser.

She took a healthy swallow of her margarita and gestured to Carl, the longtime bartender, for another one as she swung her foot in time to the music.

Who was she kidding? If she had stayed at the ranch, she wouldn't be snuggled up with a movie and a bowl of popcorn. Not when her mother and brother had company—hence her escape to The Hitching Post, so she wouldn't have to smile and nod and make nice with Erin Castro. Right this moment Erin was having dinner with her miraculous, newfound family—Elise's own mother, Helen, her brother Grant and his pregnant wife, Stephanie Julen Clifton.

Escaping the family gathering had probably been cowardly. Rude, even. Helen and John Clifton had raised her to be much more polite than that. But the truth was, she wasn't sure she was capable of spending a couple of hours making polite conversation just now, even though she liked Erin.

She couldn't blame this twisted tangle on the other woman. It wasn't Erin's fault that a nurse's error twenty-six years ago during an unusually hectic night at Thunder Canyon General Hospital and a string of mistakes had resulted in two baby girls—born on the same night to mothers sharing a room—being inadvertently switched.

Erin might have set into motion the chain of events that had led to the discovery of the hospital mistake—and the shocking truth that Elise's birth parents were a couple she had never even met until a few weeks ago—but she had only been trying to look into a mysterious claim by a relative that the truth of her birth rested somewhere in Thunder Canyon. She had come here several months ago to investigate why she looked nothing like her siblings and had finally discovered that she was in reality the child of Helen and the late John Clifton, while Elise—who had spent her lifetime thinking she knew exactly who she was and her place in the world—had been stunned to learn she was the biological child of Betty and Jack Castro.

Elise understood the other woman hadn't set out to drop an atomic bomb in her life, only to find answers. But every time Elise saw how happy her mother and Grant were now that they had found out the truth about the events of twenty-six years ago—and in effect gained another daughter and sister—Elise felt more and more like she didn't belong.

She took another healthy swallow of her drink, welcoming the warm, easy well-being that helped push away that sense of always being on the outside, looking in.

The funny thing was, she couldn't really blame Erin

for that, either. She always felt like an outsider whenever she came to town because she *was* an outsider. Oh, she had lived in Thunder Canyon through elementary and middle school. She had loved it here, had thought she would stay forever—until the horrible events of that day more than a decade ago when her father and a neighboring rancher were murdered by cattle rustlers.

She couldn't say she was exactly a stranger in town. She and her mother came back occasionally to visit family and friends. Scattered throughout the bar and grill were various people she recognized. Her family's ties here ran deep and true, especially since Grant and Stephanie had revitalized Clifton's Pride, in addition to her brother's work as general manager of the Thunder Canyon Resort.

Grant certainly belonged here. Her mother, too, even though Helen had escaped the bad memories after her husband's violent death by moving with Elise to Billings when Elise was thirteen.

Elise didn't feel the same sense of connection. She had come back temporarily with her mother for the holidays while their family absorbed the shocking developments of the last month. But she was beginning to think she might have been better off booking a month-long cruise somewhere warm and exotic and an ocean away from this Montana town and all the pain and memories it held.

The desire was reinforced when The Hitching Post door opened with a blast of wintry air. Like everybody else in the place, she instinctively looked up to see who it might be, but quickly turned back toward Lily Divine, her stomach suddenly as tangled as those wisps of material covering Lily's abundant charms.

Matt Cates.

She averted her face away from the door, mortified at the idea of him noticing her sitting here alone like some pathetic barfly.

He didn't seem to be on a date, which was odd. From the rumors she heard even after she moved away, Matt and his twin brother, Marlon, both enjoyed living up to their wild reputation.

Marlon was apparently reformed now that he was engaged to Haley. She didn't know about Matt, though.

Out of the corner of her gaze, she spotted him heading over to a booth in the corner where several other guys she vaguely recognized from school years ago had ordered pizza and a pitcher of beer.

Some of her tension eased. From his vantage point, he wouldn't have a direct line of sight to her. Maybe he wouldn't even notice her. Why would he? She had always been pretty invisible to him, other than as an annoying kid he always seemed to have to rescue.

She crossed the fingers of her left hand under the bar and reached for her third—or was it fourth?—margarita with her right.

"How'd I get so lucky to be sitting next to the prettiest girl in the place?"

Elise turned at the drawl, so close she could practically feel the hot breath puffing in her ear. She had been so busy hiding from Matt, she hadn't realized the cowboy had maneuvered his way to the bar stool next to her.

She definitely should slow down on the margaritas, since the ten gallons of Stetson cologne he must have used hadn't tipped her off to him.

"Oh. Hi." Her cheeks heated and she cursed her fair skin.

"I'm Jake. Jake Halloran."

She should just ignore him. She wasn't the sort to talk to strange men in a bar. But then, everything she knew about herself had been turned upside down in the last two weeks, so why not? It had to be marginally better than sitting here by herself.

"Hi, Jake. You from around here?"

"I'm working out at the Lazy D." His heavy-eyed gaze sharpened on her. "You sure you're old enough to be in here? You must have used a fake ID, right? Come on, you can tell me the truth."

"I—"

"Don't worry, darlin'. I won't say a word."

He smiled and mimicked turning a key at his lips. He was good-looking in a rough-edged sort of way, with tawny blond hair beneath his black Resistol and a thin, craggy, Viggo Mortenson kind of face.

She supposed she was just tipsy enough to be a little flattered at his obvious interest. Not that she had the greatest track record where men were concerned. She sighed a little. Her one and only serious relationship had been a total disaster. Kind of tough to see it any other way after the man she'd considered her first real boyfriend—and had surrendered her virginity to—introduced her to his lovely fiancée.

She'd dated on and off over the three years since

then, but most guys tended to see her as a buddy. Jake Halloran obviously didn't. Though she thought it was more than a little creepy that he would be willing to flirt with somebody he thought might be underage, she figured there was no harm in flirting back just a little.

"I appreciate that, Jake," she answered. "But I've known Carl, the bartender over there, since I took my first steps. He knows exactly how old I am and would be the first one to tan my hide if I were caught trying to pass a fake ID in The Hitching Post."

"Is that right? So how old are you?"

"Old enough," she answered pertly.

"Well, however old you are, you are about the prettiest thing I've seen in this whole town."

"Um, thanks." She forced a smile.

"How come I haven't seen you around before now?"

"I'm from out of town, here visiting family for the holidays." Or at least visiting the people she had always considered her family.

"What's your name?"

It was a simple question, really. Just about the most basic question a person could be asked. She still hesitated before answering, for a whole host of reasons.

"Elise. Elise Clifton."

The words came out almost defiantly. She *was* Elise Clifton. That's who she had been for twenty-six years, even if it turned out to be a lie.

She gestured to Carl for another margarita, even though she was usually a one-drink kind of gal.

"Well, Elise Clifton," Jake said. "This is goin' to

sound like a cheap line but what's a sweet-looking girl like you doing in a place like this all by herself?"

Now that was a very good question. She took a swallow of the new drink Carl delivered as the music shifted to a cover of a rocking Dwight Yoakam song. "Listening to the guys," she finally answered. "They're one of my favorite bands."

At just that moment, she spied Matt over Jake's shoulder. He stood at the other end of the bar, talking to a middle-aged man she didn't know.

He was so gosh-darned gorgeous, with that streaky brown hair and warm brown eyes and broad shoulders. She sighed. She'd always had more than a bit of a crush on Matt, ever since the day in first grade when he had taken down a big third-grade boy who had pushed her into a mud puddle.

Matt didn't see her as any sort of romantic interest. She knew that perfectly well. To him, she was small-for-her-age Elise Clifton, bookish and shy and clumsy, always in need of some silly rescue.

He turned in her direction and she quickly angled her body so she was hidden by the cowboy's big hat and his broad shoulders.

Jake's eyes widened with surprise at her maneuver, which also happened to put her closer to him, then she saw a gleam of appreciation spark there and he tilted his head even more closely.

"They are a mighty fine band," he agreed. "Makes you want to get up there and dance, doesn't it?"

"The bass player went to school with me," she said, trying her level best to act as if practically sitting in a stranger's lap was an everyday event. "He used to play tuba in the school band."

"Is that right? What did you play?"

"Clarinet," she answered. "I'm really good at blowing things."

He choked on his drink. It took her several beats of listening to him cough and splutter to figure out what she'd said and then she gasped. Her face flared—she wanted to sink through the floor. She was apparently a really cheap drunk. After three and a half margaritas, she excelled at unintentional double entendres.

"That's not what I meant," she exclaimed. "I really did play the clarinet. Oh!"

He laughed roughly, wiping his mouth with a napkin he'd grabbed off the bar. "I'd love to see you…play the clarinet."

Okay, she should really leave. Right now, before Jake Halloran got any ideas about checking out her embouchure.

Despite her discomfort, she laughed at her own joke but when she looked up, Lily Divine seemed to be undulating up there on the wall like a snake dancer. Elise blinked. Maybe she needed to switch to water for a while. Apparently the fourth margarita hadn't been her greatest idea.

"Hey, you wanna dance?" Jake suddenly asked. Either he was slurring his words or her ears weren't firing on all cylinders.

She considered his invitation, taking in the small dance floor that had been set up in front of the small stage where the band had now switched to a bluegrass version of Jingle Bells. Only a handful of couples were out there: an older man and woman doing a complicated Western swing like they were trying out for some television dancing show, another pair who weren't really even dancing, just bear-hugging like they were joined at the navel, and a couple about her age, dancing with a painful awkwardness she instantly pegged as a first date, even through her bleary brain.

Ordinarily she loved to dance. But since she had probably spent enough time in the Thunder Canyon spotlight the last few weeks, she decided she didn't need to be the center of attention by dancing out there in front of everyone. Everyone being primarily Matt Cates.

"I'm not much of a dancer," she lied. "Why don't we just talk? Get to know each other a little better?"

"Talking's nice." Jake grinned and put his hand on her knee. Through the material of her favorite skinny jeans, his hand felt uncomfortably hot. "Gettin' to know each other better is even nicer."

Drat Haley and her stupid rhinovirus.

She tried to subtly ease her knee away, wondering if she ought to ask Carl for a cup of coffee.

"Where are you from, Jake?" she asked a little desperately. "Originally, I mean."

"Over Butte way. My daddy had to sell off our little ranch a few years ago so I've been on my own since then. What about you?"

"Um, I live in Billings most of the time. I'm only in town for the holidays. I think I said that already."

"You did. And doesn't that work out just fine for me?"

She barely heard him. Out of the corner of her gaze,

she saw a woman in tight Wranglers and a chest-popping holiday sweater approach Matt's table and a moment later, he headed out to the dance floor with her. Elise refused to watch and shifted a little more so her would-be Romeo was blocking her from view.

He didn't seem to mind. "Hey, what do you say we get out of here? Take a little drive and see the Christmas lights?"

She might be tipsy, but she wasn't completely stupid. She wouldn't go with him, even if his breath *wasn't* strong enough to tarnish the frame on Lily's picture.

"I'd better not. I don't want to miss the music. That's the reason I'm here, after all."

Just her luck, at just that moment, the lead singer stepped up to the mike. "We're going to take fifteen, folks. Meantime you can keep dancing to the jukebox."

"What do you say? Want to at least walk outside and get some air?"

Air might be nice. Even cold air. The faster she worked the margaritas out of her system, the faster she could leave. Where she would go until the dinner party with Erin was over was a question she didn't want to consider yet.

Though she was leery about going anywhere with a man she had just met and didn't trust, how much trouble could she get into walking out into the snowy parking lot on a frigid Montana night? Anything had to be better than sitting here trying to avoid being seen.

"Sure. Let me grab my coat."

The coat and hat racks at The Hitching Post lined

the hallway on the way to the restrooms. She decided to make a quick stop at the ladies' room first to check her lipstick and maybe splash a little water on her face to clear her head.

It helped a little, but not much. When she emerged a few moments later, she found Jake lurking in the hallway.

"I thought you might be having trouble finding your coat," he murmured. For some reason, she thought that was hilarious. As if she was so stupid she couldn't recognize her own coat, for heaven's sake.

"Nope. I just stopped to fix my lipstick."

"It looks real pretty."

"Um, thanks." Maybe going outside with him wasn't such a great idea. Actually, she was beginning to think walking through The Hitching Post doors tonight ranked right up there with her worst decisions ever. Second only to her ridiculous lapse in judgment in ever agreeing to date that cheating louse Jeremy Kaiser in college.

Jake cornered her just to the edge of the row of coats. "Bet that lipstick tastes as good as it looks," he said in what he probably thought was a sexy growl. Instead, he sounded vaguely like a cat whose tail just had a close encounter with a sliding door.

He leaned in closer and she edged backward until her hands scraped the dingy wood paneling.

He dipped his head but she managed to shift her face away at the last minute. "Um, I think I changed my mind about going outside. Too cold. Let's go dance."

"I reckon we can do a pretty good tango right here," he murmured.

He tried again and she planted her palms on the chambray of his Western-cut dress shirt. "No, I really want to go dance," she said and realized her voice sounded overloud in the still-empty hallway.

Where was everybody? Didn't anybody in the whole place need to use the bathroom, for Pete's sake?

They struggled a little there in the hallway and she started to feel the first little pinch of fear when she realized she wasn't making a lick of headway against those cowboy-tough muscles.

"Come on, darlin'. A little kiss won't hurt nobody."

"I don't think so. I don't know you."

His face hardened and she wondered why she ever thought he looked a little like Viggo. More like Ichabod Crane. "You sure knew me well enough to be all snuggly over at the bar," he snarled.

"Hey," she exclaimed when his hand slid behind her to hold her in place. She pushed at the pearl buttons on his shirt. "Let go."

"Come on. Just a kiss. That's all."

"No!" She wriggled and squirmed but was faced with the grim realization that her 110-pound, five-foot-four frame was no match for somebody who wrangled tons of Angus cattle for a living. "Let me go!"

"Looks to me like the lady's not interested, Halloran."

The familiar steely voice managed to pierce both her sudden attack of nerves and her muzzy head.

She swallowed a curse. Matt. Her miserable night just needed this. Her face blazed and she knew she must be more red than a shiny glass Christmas ornament. Of every single person out in the crowded bar, why did he have to be the next one who happened into the hallway to come to her rescue?

Chapter Two

Matt stood a few feet away from them in the otherwise empty hallway, an almost bored look on his rugged features.

Jake Halloran had muscles, but he was no match for Matt, who helped run his family's construction business. He loomed over the other man, big and dark and dangerous.

"This ain't none of your concern, Cates," the wrangler currently trying to wrangle *her* snarled. "You don't know what you're talkin' about, so just walk on by."

"I don't think so." Matt stepped forward, looking tough and dangerous and heartstoppingly gorgeous. Elise slammed her eyes shut.

"Hey, Elise."

She opened them to find him watching her, a slight

smile playing around his mouth. She certainly wouldn't be wriggling and squirming like a lassoed calf if *that* mouth had been the one coming at her.

"Hi," she whispered. She was never drinking again. Never drinking and certainly never talking to strange men in bars again.

"Let's let the lady decide, why don't we?" Matt said calmly. "Elise, you want me to walk on by and leave the both of you to whatever was going on here that you didn't particularly appear to be enjoying a minute ago?"

What kind of choice was that? She didn't want him here, but she certainly didn't want to be the star attraction in octopus cage fighting anymore.

"No," she whispered, then cleared her throat when she heard that pitiful rasp. "No," she repeated more firmly. "Don't go."

"That sounded pretty clear-cut to me, Halloran. The lady isn't interested. Better luck next time."

Matt reached around the cowboy to grab her arm and extricate her from yet another humiliating situation. With a tangled mixture of relief and trepidation, she reached to take his hand.

She wasn't sure exactly what happened next. One moment she was stuck to the cowboy's side, the next Matt had her elbow firmly in his grip and was leading her away.

"Come on, Elise. Let's get you something to eat."

They took maybe three steps away from the situation when the wrangler grabbed her other arm and yanked her back. Pain seared from her shoulder to her fingers and Elise gave an instinctive cry.

Why in *Hades* hadn't she just put on her big-girl panties and stayed at the ranch to deal with Erin? Anything would be better than this. She did not want to be here right now, caught in a tug-of-war between two tough, dangerous men.

Something dark and hot flared in Matt's expression as he eyed the other man. "You're going to want to let go of her arm now," he said in a low voice, all the more ominous for its calmness.

"I saw her first," Jake muttered, just as if she were the last slice of apple pie in the bakery display case.

Elise managed to wrench her wrist out of his grasp and after a moment, Matt continued leading her back toward the bar, but apparently Jake didn't get the message.

"I saw her *first*," he said more insistently and shoved his way in front of them to block their path.

A muscle flexed in Matt's firm jaw. He certainly didn't look like the kind of guy *she* would want to tangle with. "Come on, Halloran. Take it easy. The lady wasn't interested, but I'm sure there are plenty more back at the bar who will be."

"Want this one," he said, reaching for her arm again. This time Matt stopped him with a sharp block from his own arm. In the tussle for her appendage, Matt shoved the wrangler away. Halloran stumbled back, but came up swinging with a powerful right hook that connected hard with Matt's eye.

Elise gasped and jerked away from both men in time to evade Matt's defensive punch in return.

And that was it. Halloran leaped on him, yelling and swinging.

"Fight!" somebody yelled inside the bar, resulting in a mad rush of people into the narrow hallway. The only thing patrons of The Hitching Post liked better than a good band was a rousing brawl.

Matt's buddies at his booth joined in to pull the wrangler off. As soon as he was clear, he grabbed Elise and pushed out toward the nearest booth and out of harm's way, but apparently the cowboy had friends at The Hitching Post, too, and soon it was a free-for-all that spilled from the restroom hallway into the main room of the bar.

Everybody seemed to be having a grand old time until Carl took matters into his own hands.

"Knock it off, you idiots," the bartender yelled out, working the pump action of an old Remington shotgun, just like he was out of some cheesy old Western like the kind her dad used to love to watch.

Another voice joined in. "What the hell is going on here? Who started this?"

About a dozen hands pointed toward Matt and Jake, roughly equally divided between the two, as Elise recognized Joe Morales, a Thunder Canyon sheriff's deputy, who didn't look happy to have his dinner interrupted when he was obviously off duty.

"Cates. Should have known you'd be involved," he grumbled, his brushy salt-and-pepper mustache quivering. "What the hell happened?"

Since he seemed to be focusing on the two of them, the rest of the crowd seemed happy to slip away from any scrutiny and return to their drinks and their food. Elise really wanted to join them all and started easing away, but Matt pinned her into place beside him with a glare, as if this was all *her* fault.

"Sumbitch stole my girl." A thin trail of blood spilled out of the corner of Jake Halloran's mouth and he wiped at it with a napkin.

The deputy frowned at Elise. "You his girl?"

She shook her head, grateful she was still sitting down in the booth when the room spun a little. "I just met him tonight."

"You're Elise Clifton, aren't you? Grant's sister?"

Wouldn't her brother just love to hear about this little escapade? She couldn't wait to try explaining to Grant why she had let herself get cornered in an empty hallway by a drunk cowboy. "Yes."

"Well, Ms. Clifton, the guy seems to think there was more to it than a little chatting at the bar."

"He's wrong," she said, then was appalled at the note of belligerence in her voice. Must be the margaritas. She normally was not a belligerent person. Just another reason she needed to swear off drinking for a long time.

"We were only talking, Deputy Morales," she went on in what she hoped was a much more cooperative tone of voice. "I met him maybe half an hour ago. We talked about walking outside for some fresh air while the band was taking a break. I came back here to get my coat and he just…kissed me."

She drew in a shaky breath, more mortified than she

ever remembered feeling in her life. Even more embarrassed than the time she had been bucked off by her horse in the junior rodeo for Thunder Canyon Days when she was eleven and Matt had been the first one to her side.

"I tried to tell him I wasn't interested but he didn't listen," she said. "Then Matt came into the hallway and saw I was having a tough time convincing him to stop, so he stepped in to help me and Jake hit him."

"How much have you had to drink, Ms. Clifton?"

She looked down at the speckled Formica tabletop then back up, drawing a breath and hoping she sounded more coherent than she felt. "Not so much that I don't know how to be perfectly clear when I'm saying no to a man, sir."

"That what happened?" he asked Halloran. "Did she say no?"

"I heard her say no, Joe," Matt said. "Loud and clear."

"I don't believe I asked you," the deputy growled. Elise suddenly remembered he had a younger sister who had once carried a very public torch for Matt back in Matt's younger, wilder days when bar fights probably weren't an uncommon occurrence.

"Did the girl say no?" he asked Jake again.

"Well, yeah. But you know how women can be."

The deputy gave him a long, disgusted look, then turned back to Elise. "Do you want to press charges for assault?"

She gave him a horrified look. "No. Heavens no! It was just a misunderstanding." Yes, the man had been wrong to paw her, especially when she'd made it clear she didn't want him to. But she had been wrong to flirt with him back at the bar, to use him only so she could hide from Matt.

"What about you, Cates? You want to press charges?"

Matt shook his dark head. "I know how things can get out of hand in the heat of the moment."

"Fine. All of you get out of here, then, so I can go back to my wife and my steak. Can you make sure she makes it back to Clifton's Pride okay?" he asked Matt.

Matt gave her a look she couldn't decipher, then nodded.

The moment the deputy ushered Jake over to the other Lazy D cowboys who had come to his rescue, Elise rushed back to the hallway, grabbed her red peacoat off the rack and twisted her scarf around her neck. She had to escape. What a nightmare. As if she needed more gossip about her flying through town.

She heard someone call her name but she didn't stop, only pushed through the front door out into the cold night.

The streets of Thunder Canyon glittered with brightly colored Christmas lights. They blinked at her from storefronts and the few houses she could see from here. A light snow drifted down, the flakes plump and soft. Away from the front door, she lifted her face for a moment to feel their light, wet kisses on her face.

She found a strange sort of comfort at the realization that she'd been seeing the same holiday decorations in Thunder Canyon since she was a girl. Her entire life may have changed in the last few weeks, but some things remained constant.

"You're not thinking about driving in your condition, are you?"

She opened her eyes, somehow not very surprised to find Matt standing a few feet away, looking big and dark and dangerous in a shearling-lined ranch coat. His eye was beginning to swell and color up and he had a thin cut on his cheek she very much feared would leave a scar.

"Thinking about it," she admitted.

"Sorry, El, but I can't let you do that. You heard what the deputy said. I need to take you home."

"And how are you going to stop me?" she asked, with more of that unexpected belligerence.

He smiled suddenly and she blinked at the brilliance of it in the dark night. That must be why she was taken completely off guard when he reached for her purse. After a moment of fishing through the contents, he pulled her keys out, dangled them out for a moment, and then pocketed them neatly in his coat.

"I can give you a ride back to the ranch and find somebody later to take your car home. Face it, Elise, you're in no shape to drive."

She couldn't go back to Clifton's Pride yet. Just the thought of walking inside the ranch house in her condition made her queasy.

She didn't need to see that same wary look in everyone's eyes she'd been dealing with since before Thanksgiving, as if she were somebody who had been given some kind of terminal diagnosis or something. Her mother hugged her at the oddest moments and Grant and his wife, Stephanie, went out of their way to include her in conversations.

She especially didn't want to show up tipsy when Erin was there in all her perfection, the daughter they *should* have had.

"I don't want to go home yet," she whispered, grimly aware the words sounded even more pathetic spoken aloud.

"No?"

"Not yet. I'll only be in the way. My...my mother and Grant have...well...guests for dinner."

He gave her another of those long, considering looks and she could feel herself flush, certain he could guess what—or rather whom—she meant.

"Want to go back inside?"

She shook her head. "I don't think I need to see the inside of The Hitching Post for a while."

Or ever again.

"Fair enough. Do you want to go grab a bite to eat somewhere? I'm sure we can find somewhere still open."

"Not really."

He gave a half laugh. "Well, I'm running out of options. You'll freeze to death if you sit out here in the parking lot for another hour or two until your head clears."

"I know."

After another pause, he sighed. "My place is just a block or two away. If you want to, I can get cleaned up and fix you something to eat and we can hang there until you think the coast is clear back at Clifton's Pride."

She hated that he had to come to her rescue, just like when they were kids. She had been a clumsy kid and it seemed like every time she fell, he had been right there to help her back up, brush off the dirt, gather her books, whatever she needed.

From the time he had fought two schoolyard bullies bigger than he was—and won—he had been stepping in to protect her from the world.

She was twenty-six years old. Surely it was high time she found the gumption to fight her own battles. Still, the idea of somebody else taking care of her for a few minutes sounded heavenly.

"Don't you ever get tired of rescuing me?" she asked.

Instead of answering, he laughed and tucked a strand of hair behind her ear. His hand was warm in the cold December air and she wanted to lean into him, close her eyes and stay there forever.

"Come on. Let's get you out of the snow."

Chapter Three

Though Matt only lived a few blocks from The Hitching Post, Elise dozed off beside him in his pickup truck before he reached his house—a small, run-down cottage on Cedar Street he had purchased a few months back to rehab in his spare time away from his work at Cates Construction.

Before the first snow a few months earlier, he'd rushed to put new shingles on and managed a new coat of white paint and green shutters. From the outside, the place looked fresh and tidy.

Inside was an entirely different story.

He thought about driving around for a while to let her sleep off the alcohol in her system, but he had a feeling she probably needed food more than sleep. Back in the day when he used to enjoy the wild weekend here or there, that's what always helped him most.

He pulled into his driveway and put his truck in gear, though he left his engine running to keep the heater blowing. He shifted his gaze to her and shook his head.

Elise Clifton.

She was still as sweet and pretty as she had always been, blonde and petite, with delicate features, a slim little nose and her cupid's bow of a mouth.

She always looked a year or two younger than the rest of their grade. Now she probably considered that a good thing, but when they were kids, he knew she had hated being mistaken for a younger kid.

Maybe that was why she always stirred up all his protective instincts. She was right, it seemed like he was always coming to her rescue. He hadn't minded. Not one damn bit. He only had brothers—a twin and two older ones—and didn't know much about dealing with girls back when he was a kid. But his father had taught them all that a guy was supposed to watch out for those who were smaller than him.

Elise certainly fit the bill—then, and now. She looked small and fragile with her blond hair fanned out on the pickup's upholstery and her bottom lip snagged between her teeth.

Elise had always seemed a little more in need of rescuing than others. Even before the terrible events when she was thirteen, something about her seemed to stir up all his protective impulses.

Her long lashes fluttered now as she blinked her eyes

open. For a brief instant, she smiled at him, her eyes the soft, breathtaking blue of the Montana sky on an early summer morning. As he gazed at her, he felt as if he'd just taken a hit to the gut from a three-hundred-pound linebacker.

He drew in a breath, trying to shake off the unexpected sensation. This was Elise, he reminded himself. Little Elise Clifton, whose junior-rodeo, barrel-racing belt buckle had nearly been bigger than she was.

Except she wasn't little. She hadn't been in a long, long time. Though still petite, he couldn't help but notice she was soft and curvy in all the right places.

"Feeling better?" he spoke mostly to distract himself.

Her brow furrowed a little, as if she were trying to figure that out herself. After a moment, she nodded a little shyly, a trace of color on her cheeks. "Actually, I think I am. At least there's only one of you."

"Until Marlon shows up," he joked about his identical twin, and was rewarded with her sweet-sounding laugh.

"I hope he's with Haley right now, tucking her in and bringing her tissues and chicken soup. She and I were supposed to have a girls' night out to see the band at The Hitching Post together tonight but she bailed on me at the last minute."

She sat up and stretched a little and he tried not to notice how her sweater beneath her unbuttoned coat hugged those soft curves. "Since I was already there and…well, didn't really want to go home yet, I decided to stay and listen to the band."

Ah. That explained why she'd been sitting by herself at the bar. He had spied her the moment he walked in and had been keeping an eye on the cowboy she'd been sitting beside. At first, he thought maybe they'd been on a date. The little spark of inappropriate jealousy had come out of nowhere, taking him completely by surprise.

When she walked down the hall toward the ladies' room, he had watched the cowboy follow her. When neither of them emerged after a moment, he'd gone looking for her. And just in time.

"Poor Haley," he said now. "Being sick bites anytime, but especially at Christmas. Still, I'm sure Marlon loves the chance to baby her. He's crazy about her."

"He'd better be," she said darkly. He hid a smile at the belligerent tone he'd noticed her adopting earlier. He didn't know how much she'd had to drink. With her small frame, it probably wasn't much, but he definitely recognized the signs of somebody on the tipsy side.

"Let's get you inside and find you something to eat."

"I'm really not hungry."

"Humor me, okay?"

After a moment, she shrugged and reached for the passenger-side door handle. He climbed out of the truck and hurried around the front of the pickup. His work truck was high off the ground so he reached inside and grabbed her hand to help her to the ground.

Her fingers felt small and cool inside his and when her high-heeled boots hit the ground, she wobbled a little. He reached out to steady her and found he was strangely reluctant to release her.

He held her, gazing into those blue eyes far longer than he should have while the fat snowflakes drifted down to settle in her hair and cling to her cheeks.

He hadn't seen her much over the years since she and her mother moved away from Thunder Canyon. Last time was probably over the summer when she'd come for a visit and he had ended up pulling over to help her change a flat tire.

Every time he saw her, he was struck again how lovely she was.

He had missed her, he suddenly realized. More than he ever could have imagined.

She shivered suddenly and the delicate motion jolted him back to his senses. "Let's get you inside."

"Thanks," she murmured.

He gripped her arm so she didn't slip on the skiff of snow covering his sidewalk as he led the way up the porch. He twisted the key in the lock and was greeted by one well-mannered bark that made him smile.

As soon as he opened the door, a brown shape snuffled excitedly and headed toward them. Elise took a quick, instinctive step backward on the porch, wobbling a little again on her dressy boots.

He reached for her arm again, feeling the heat of her beneath the red wool coat she wore. "Sorry about that. I should have warned you. Tootsie, sit."

His chocolate Labrador immediately planted her haunches on the polished wood floor of the entry, her tail wagging like crazy.

Elise reached down to pet her head. "Tootsie?"

He winced. "When she was a puppy, she looked like a big, fat Tootsie Roll. My mom named her."

Tootsie waited patiently until he gave her the signal to come ahead, then she hurried to his side and nudged his leg for a little love.

"She's beautiful, Matt."

"The sweetest dog I've ever had, aren't you, baby?"

She snuffled in response and he obediently scratched her favorite spot, right behind her left ear.

He loved having a dog to keep him company. When the weather wasn't so cold, she rode with him to construction sites. After the cold weather set in, his favorite evenings were spent at home watching a basketball game with her curled up at his feet.

Used to be Marlon would join them but these days his twin had better ways to spend his time.

Matt supposed it was only natural that lately Tootsie's company didn't seem quite enough anymore, especially since it seemed like everybody he knew was pairing up.

"How long have you lived here?" Elise asked.

He shifted his attention from the dog to his house and winced again at its sorry shape. The place was a work in progress. He had stripped years worth of ugly wallpaper layers, down to the lath and plaster. He'd finished mudding the walls a few weeks earlier but had been so busy rushing his crew to finish Connor McFarlane's grand lodge in time for Christmas, he hadn't had time to paint.

At least the kitchen and bathroom were relatively

presentable. He had started with the kitchen, actually, installing hand-peeled cabinets, custom tile floors and gleaming new appliances.

He had also taken out the wall of a tiny bedroom to expand the bathroom into one big space and he was particularly satisfied with the triple heads in the tile shower and the deep soaking tub.

But he couldn't exactly entertain his unexpected guest in his bathroom. Maybe he should have spent a little more time working on the more public areas of the house.

"I've got lots of plans but I have to fit the work around the jobs I'm doing with my dad," he said.

She nodded. "That's right. I heard you were working for Cates Construction these days. Do you like it?"

He was never sure how to answer that question. Most of the time, he was only too aware of the subtext behind the question. *You really dropped out of law school to work construction? Couldn't hack it, huh?*

That hadn't been the truth at all. His grades had been fine after his first year of law school. Better than fine. Great, actually. He'd been in the top ten percent of his class and had fully intended going back for his second year—until he realized after he came home to Montana for the summer that he was much happier out at a work site with his dad, covered in the satisfying sweat of putting in a hard day's labor, than he'd ever been in a classroom.

"I do like it. There's always a new challenge and it's great to watch something go from blueprints to completion, like the McFarlane Lodge."

"Haley told me about that. It sounds huge."

"It is. More than 10,000 square feet. It's been a fun project but a little time consuming. That's why I only have bits and pieces of time to work on this place. This is the third house in town I've rehabbed on my own."

She cast her gaze around the room. "Um, it looks good."

He smiled at her obvious lie. "No, it doesn't. Everything's a mess out here. As soon as we wrap up the McFarlane Lodge, I'll have more time for the finish work here. But come on back to the kitchen and see what I've done there. I'd love a woman's perspective."

Surprise flashed in her eyes. "Mine?"

"You see any other women around?"

"Not right this very moment," she muttered. "I'm sure that's not typical for you."

He shouldn't be irritated by her words but he was. Yeah, he'd been wild in his younger days. Not as wild as Marlon, maybe, but he'd had his moments. How long and hard did a man have to work to shake off a wild reputation?

"Come on back," he said again and led the way through the compact cottage to the kitchen.

When she saw the room, the shocked admiration on her features more than made up for the dig about his reputation.

She did a full three-sixty, taking in the slim jeweled pendant lights over the work island, the stainless-steel, professional stove, the long row of paned windows over the dining area.

"Wow! You really did all this by yourself?"

"You sound surprised. Should I be insulted by that?"

She made a face. "I guess I just never realized you were such a…what's the word? I can't think. Artisan, I guess."

"Nothing so grand as that," he protested. "I'm just a construction worker."

She slicked a hand over the marble countertop and he was suddenly entranced by the sight of her long, slim fingers sliding along his work.

He cleared his throat. "How does pasta sound? I've got some lemon tarragon sauce in the fridge I can heat up while I throw a pot of water on to boil."

"You cook, too? I guess with a kitchen like this, you must."

"Not much," he was forced to admit. "The kitchen's for whoever eventually buys the place. I've got a few specialties and know enough so I don't starve. That's about it. My mom sent over the pasta sauce. She thinks I live on fast food and TV dinners."

"I don't want you to go to any work."

"How much effort does it take to boil a pot of water on the stove and push a few buttons on the microwave? Have a seat. If you'd rather go in and watch something on TV, the family room isn't in too bad of shape, as long as you don't mind a few exposed wires."

"I'll stay here. Could I have a drink of water?"

"I can make coffee. That would clear your head faster."

"Water is okay for now."

He pulled a tumbler out of the cabinet by the sink

and dispensed ice and cold, filtered water from the re-frigerator. When he handed it to her, she took a seat at one of the stools around the work island. Tootsie, always happy for someone new to love, settled beside her and Elise smiled a little and reached down to pet her before the dog curled up on the kitchen floor.

"Maybe you ought to put something on that black eye, don't you think?"

How had he managed to block out the throbbing from both his eye and his cheek where Halloran had gotten off a cheap shot? She was a powerful distraction, appar-ently. "Right. Let me get the fight washed off me first and then I'll fix you something to eat."

"Do you need help?"

He thought of those fingers, cool and light on his skin, and felt his body stir with interest. This was Elise, he reminded himself. Not some bar babe looking for a good time.

"I think I can handle it," he finally answered. He wasn't sure he trusted himself around her right now. "Hang tight. I'll be back in a minute."

It took him about ten to wash away the blood, most of it belonging to the idiot who had mauled her, and to change his shirt. When he returned to the kitchen, some of the tension had eased from her features. She was leaf-ing through a design book he'd left on the kitchen desk and she looked sweet and relaxed and comfortable.

As if she belonged there.

She looked up and he watched her gaze slide to the bandage he'd applied just under his colorful eye.

"Does it hurt?"

"I've had worse, believe me."

That didn't seem to ease her concern. "You could have been really hurt. He might have damaged your vision."

"He didn't. I'm fine."

She closed the book, her fine-boned features tight and unhappy. "I'm really sorry about…everything. I feel so stupid."

"Why? You didn't do anything wrong except maybe pass the time of day with a cowboy who'd had a few too many."

"I can't really blame him for getting the wrong idea," she admitted. "I might have…acted more interested in him than I really was. If you want the truth, I was using him to hide from you."

He raised his eyebrows. "Why would you need to hide from me?"

She suddenly looked as if she wished she'd never said anything. "I was embarrassed about being there by myself. It's not something I usually do."

"I'm glad you were there," he said as he headed to the refrigerator for the sauce. "Except for your little episode with the jerk, it's great to see you. So are you back in Thunder Canyon to stay?"

She sighed and sounded so forlorn that Tootsie must have sensed it. She nuzzled her leg. "I don't know. Everything's in…limbo. My mother wanted to come home for the holidays and begged me to come with her so I took a temporary leave from my job until the new year. After that, I don't know what I'll do."

He really hoped she would decide to stay. He liked

having her around. He started to say so but she spoke before he could get the words out.

"I guess you heard about my…about what happened twenty-six years ago."

"Who in town hasn't?"

Her sigh this time sounded even more forlorn and he cursed himself for his tactless response.

"Sorry. Was that the wrong thing to say?"

"I really hate having everyone gossiping about me. I hated it after my dad's murder and I hate it more now. Everything is such a mess."

He couldn't begin to imagine what she must be going through. "How are you holding up?"

"Not too great," she confessed softly.

He set down the box of pasta he'd just pulled from the cupboard and crossed to give her a reassuring squeeze on the shoulder.

Instead of comforting her, as he'd intended, his gesture made her big blue eyes brim with tears.

"My mom wants the family together for Christmas. Everyone, including Erin."

"And that's a problem?"

She sighed. "I feel like I don't even belong at Clifton's Pride anymore."

He stared. "You most certainly *do* belong at Clifton's Pride! It's your home and the Cliftons are your family. Why would you feel otherwise, even for a moment?"

"I'm not a Clifton. Not really. If not for a quirk of fate and a moment's mistake by a nurse, I never would have known any one of them. I'm not a Clifton. But I'm not really a Castro, either. I barely know those people. I don't know who I am."

A tear brimming in her eyes dripped over and slid down the side of her nose and his heart broke.

He grabbed a tissue box and couldn't resist the compulsion to pull her into his arms. She felt small and feminine and he wanted to hold tight and take on all her demons for her.

"You're the same person you've always been. You're Elise Clifton, daughter of John and Helen and sister to Grant. Blood or not, that's who you are."

"I wish it were that easy."

"Why isn't it? They're your family."

She frowned. "They're not my parents! I don't belong in Thunder Canyon at all!"

A dozen arguments swarmed through his head—he hadn't been in law school without reason. But then, she wasn't a hostile witness on the stand, either.

"So blood and genetics is everything? According to your reasoning, anybody who's been adopted into a family should always feel like an outsider."

"I wasn't adopted!" she exclaimed. "I was switched for their real daughter. For the child Helen and John should have had. They didn't choose to be stuck with me. My whole life is a mistake! *I'm* a mistake."

"Do you really think that's what your mother and Grant think?"

"I don't know. They're so happy about Erin," she whispered.

Her tears started flowing in earnest now and she added a few sobs in there to really twist the knife.

Nice, Cates, he thought. *Take a vulnerable woman who has already had a rough night and reduce her to tears.* He had definitely lost his touch.

"Hey. Easy now. Come on." He pulled her back into his arms.

"I'm sorry. I'm so sorry." She sniffled.

"For what? Being human? Anybody would be upset."

"Oh, I'm making a big mess of your shirt and you just changed it for a clean one," she wailed.

He tightened his arms. "No worries. I've got a good washing machine."

His words only seemed to set her off again and Matt held her, hating this helpless feeling. With no sisters and a mother who rarely lost her cool in front of her boys, his experience with crying women was extremely limited. This was a novel experience, trying to offer comfort instead of instinctively seeking any handy escape route.

She clutched his waist as if he was the only thing keeping her from floating away on her wild emotions, her cheek pressed against his chest. Her hair smelled like fresh raspberries just plucked from his mama's garden behind their house and he inhaled, doing his best to ignore how soft and curvy she felt in his arms and feeling powerless to do anything but hold her.

He moved into his half-finished family room where he could sit down on the sofa, pulling her with him.

After a few moments, her intense sobs quieted. She took a few slow, hitching breaths and he could feel the shudders against him subside.

With vast relief, he felt her regain control until some

time later when she eased slightly away from him, though she didn't seem any more eager to leave the shelter of his arms than he was to let her go.

"This is the single most embarrassing night of my life," she finally said, her cheeks flaring with color. "Apparently, I'm a maudlin drunk. Who knew?"

He laughed a little roughly, still unnerved by the intensity of his attraction to her, which somehow far outweighed all those protective impulses.

Elise always had the ability to make him laugh, he remembered. She had a funny, quirky sense of humor and he remembered back in school feeling privileged to be among the few she revealed it to.

"I haven't cried once since…well, since Erin told us all what she suspected."

"Then you are probably long overdue, aren't you?"

She said nothing for a long moment and then she smiled at him and he felt like he was seeing his first taste of springtime after weeks of fog and gloom.

Even with her reddened eyes and tear-stained cheeks, she was beautiful. He gazed at her upturned face a long moment, then with a strange sense of destiny or fate or inevitability—he wasn't sure—he leaned down and pressed his mouth to that smile.

Chapter Four

Elise froze at the first warm touch of his mouth. He tasted delicious, like fresh-baked cinnamon cookies, and his arms around her seemed the safest place in the universe.

She couldn't quite believe this was happening and wondered for a moment if she was hallucinating. No, she hadn't had quite *that* much to drink. She wasn't sure about a lot of things but she knew that, at least.

Matt Cates, who had never looked twice at her all these years, really was kissing her, holding her, like he couldn't get enough.

Elise would have laughed at the sheer, unexpected wonder of it if she wasn't so preoccupied with the sexy things his mouth was doing to hers.

This all seemed so surreal. She wasn't exactly a

femme fatale. Most guys tended to think of her like the girl next door, somebody sweet and fairly innocent. Blame it on her blond hair or the blue eyes or her small stature. She didn't know exactly what, she only knew that she wasn't the kind of girl men considered for a quick fling.

Now, twice in one night in the space of only an hour or so, she found herself in a man's arms. Not that the two things were in any way comparable. Kissing Matt Cates was a whole different experience than trying to fight off Jake Halloran in the hallway outside the ladies' room at The Hitching Post.

Then, she had been doing everything she could to avoid the man and wriggle away from him. With Matt, she had absolutely no desire to escape. She wanted to stay right here forever, where she was warm and safe.

She should be curling up behind the sofa with a blanket over her head. Even as he kissed her, she couldn't shake her lingering embarrassment when she remembered her emotional breakdown.

Definitely must have been the margaritas. Why else would she spill everything to Matt when she hadn't talked to another soul about her emotional turmoil over learning of the hospital mistake? She hadn't told her mother or Grant or even Stephanie, Grant's wife, who along with Haley Anderson had been her closest friend when they were kids.

Matt only had to show her a little sympathy in those brown eyes and she started blubbering all over him.

Her stomach muscles quivered as he shifted his mouth over hers. What was the matter with her? After all these years of wondering what it might be like to kiss him, she finally had her chance and she was wasting the moment being embarrassed about the events leading up to this. Was she completely insane?

She leaned into that hard, solid chest and opened her mouth for his kiss. He made a sexy little sound in his throat that rippled down her spine as if he'd run his thumb from the base of her neck to her tailbone.

He wrapped his arms more tightly around her and slid his tongue inside her mouth and she forgot everything else but Matt.

She slid her hands in his hair. Funny, she might have expected his thick dark hair to be short, coarse, but it felt silky and decadent against her skin.

Time seemed to shift and slide and she had no idea how long they stayed there on his sofa, wrapped together. She only knew she didn't want him to stop. Matt suddenly felt like the only solid, secure thing she had to hang on to since Erin Castro shook the foundations of her world.

His hand burned through the cotton of her sweater and she ached for closer contact. As if in answer to some unspoken request, his hand slid beneath her sweater and glided to the small of her back. She shivered at the heat of him and murmured his name.

Well, that was a mistake, she thought as he froze. Next time she would keep her lovesick murmurings to herself.

He wrenched his mouth away and she felt even more like an idiot. His breathing was ragged and he looked like he'd just been kicked off a prize bull.

He stared at her for a long moment, then raked a hand through his hair. He didn't move, though, and she was still sprawled against him.

"I'm sorry, Elise. That was the last thing you needed, another stupid cowboy pawing you."

"Was it?" she murmured.

"Yes! You're upset and vulnerable and I completely took advantage of that."

"No, you didn't." She was exhausted suddenly, her muscles loose and fluid, as if his kiss had been the only thing keeping her upright. "I'm glad you kissed me. You're a great kisser. All the girls used to say so. I'm glad I finally had the chance to find out. You really were. Great, I mean."

He gave her a skeptical look but she thought she saw a hint of color over his cheekbones. She was too tired to know for sure, though. She just wanted to close her eyes and ease into sleep like she was sliding into sun-warmed water.

"I never did rustle up something for you to eat."

She opened one eye. "I'm not hungry. Do you mind if we stay here like this for a minute?"

He looked startled for only a moment, then shook his head. "What man with a brain in his head would mind having a chance to hold a pretty girl for a while longer?"

She smiled, though the last remaining rational part of her brain was sending out a whole host of warning signals. Matthew Cates was exactly the sort of man who could make a woman completely lose her head.

She was definitely going to have to take care around him.

The thought slid through her mind but she pushed it away. She wouldn't worry about a little detail like that. Not right now. For now, she only wanted to stay right here, savoring the warmth of his arms around her and the steady rhythm of his breathing, and indulging in this rare, precious moment of peace.

It was her last thought for some time.

This should have been the perfect way to spend a December Friday night. The lights on his Christmas tree glistened brightly and through the window, he could see those plump snowflakes still drifting down.

When Elise had first fallen asleep, he had taken a chance and reached with his free hand for the remote. Somehow he had managed to turn the TV on low without waking her and had turned to one of the digital music stations offered by his satellite provider, this one playing soft, jazzy holiday music.

Matt shifted on the sofa. His legs tingled and he was pretty sure he'd lost all feeling in one arm.

He didn't mind any of that. What worried him was this unaccustomed tenderness coiling through him as he held the slight woman in his arms.

He had always cared about Elise and considered her a friend. Maybe he'd been more protective of her than most of his friends over the years, in part because she'd been small for her age and had appeared delicate, even if she really wasn't, and in part, of course, because of the terrible event in her family when she was still a girl—her father's brutal murder.

A desire to watch out for her was one thing. This desire for *her*—to taste her and touch her and explore every inch of that delectable skin—stunned him to the core.

He had never been so aroused by a simple kiss. If he hadn't suddenly remembered that she'd had a little too much to drink, he wasn't sure just how far he might have let their kiss progress.

Just remembering her sweet response—those breathy sighs, the trembling of her hands in his hair—sent a shaft of heat through him now.

He tightened his arms around her. What a hell of a mess. He didn't want to hurt a sweet girl like Elise, but his track record at relationships wasn't the greatest. He usually leaned toward women who preferred to keep things casual and that was exactly what he told himself he wanted. Fun, easy, no strings.

He thought briefly of Christine. She was the perfect example. The last thing she wanted from him was a serious commitment. The only reason they started seeing each other in the first place was because neither of them was romantically interested in the other. She wanted to avoid a persistent ex-boyfriend and he wanted to escape his mother's transparent matchmaking attempts.

He had enjoyed taking Christine around town for the last couple of months and they had a good time together, but the few experimental kisses they'd shared just to see if things might progress in some sort of natural order had left both of them shaking their heads and wondering why they just didn't spark the magic in each other.

Christine was far more his usual type than Elise. His few long-term girlfriends had each been dark-haired and tall like her, funny and social.

Elise couldn't be more different from what he had always considered his usual taste, yet he'd never known a kiss as explosive and stirring as theirs, or this soft, easy tenderness flowing through him, just from holding a woman in his arms.

He shifted on the sofa and finally drew his legs up along the length of it, sliding as far as he could to the side to make room for both of them. She murmured something in her sleep then nestled against him, her arm around his waist.

Her straight blond hair reflected the Christmas lights and he watched them for a moment, then closed his eyes. He would let her sleep for a little while until the effects of the alcohol she'd consumed were out of her system and then he would take her back to Clifton's Pride.

He was only thinking of her, he told himself. Not about how terrifyingly perfect she felt in his arms.

So much for good intentions.

When Matt awoke, Elise was still asleep snugged up against him, her arm across his chest, her hair brushing his chin and one of her legs entwined with his.

As he slid back to consciousness, he became aware of her first, small and soft against him. Not a bad way to wake up, he thought, with the sweet scent of raspberries surrounding him and a beautiful woman in his arms—and then he heard a little well-mannered whine and noticed Tootsie stretched out in front of the door, waiting to go out, something she usually only did first thing in the morning.

He shifted his gaze to the window. That couldn't be right, could it? It looked as if the first pink rays of dawn were sneaking through the slats of his window blind. Had they really slept here all night?

He was going to have a crick in his neck all day from sleeping like this and he could only hope he would regain feeling in his arm one day. Working construction might be difficult if he didn't have the use of his right arm.

Tootsie whined again and Elise made a soft little sound in her sleep and he decided all his discomforts didn't matter—a small price to pay for the pleasure of holding her.

As he watched, her eyelashes fluttered against her skin and a moment later her eyes opened. She gazed at him for a long moment and her brow furrowed.

"Matt? What are you…"

The words were barely out before she groaned. "Ow," she muttered and squeezed her temples.

He suddenly remembered her excess the night before and winced in sympathy.

"Headache?"

She sat up and opened one eye to glare balefully at him. Her hair stuck up a bit on one side and her cheek was creased with a funny little pattern from the material of his sweater but he still thought she was just about the prettiest thing he'd ever seen.

"Headache," she groaned. "That's one word for it. If you like understatements. I don't suppose you've got coffee?"

"Sorry. I've been a little preoccupied all night."

She looked at him and then at the couch and color rose up her cheeks in a rosy tide. "I fell asleep."

"We both did. I hadn't planned a sleepover. Sorry about that."

She looked at the pale light outside the window with something akin to panic. "What time is it?"

He glanced at the clock above the gas fireplace. "Early. Looks like it's not quite six. I need to put the dog out."

"Oh. Of course."

He winced a little as he stood on numb legs but still managed to make it to the door without falling over. A few more inches had fallen in the night, but not enough to be more than an annoyance. Tootsie bounded out when he opened the door and he turned back to find Elise looking distressed.

"I've been gone all night. Mom must be frantic. And Grant is going to kill me."

He had a feeling if Grant had *anyone* on his hit list, Matt's name would be right there at the top after last night.

"You're twenty-six years old, Elise. Surely you've been out all night before."

"Of course I have." She spoke the words with more than a trace of defiance. "But not when I'm staying with my mother and my brother. Or at least not without letting them know I'll be late. Maybe they'll just think I stayed over at Haley's."

He sighed. "When I let Tootsie back in, I'll run a comb through my hair and then I'll take you back to Clifton's Pride. We'll just explain what happened. I took you home to feed you after we left The Hitching Post and we both fell asleep."

"I'm sure that will go over just great."

"It's the truth. Or most of it, anyway."

She pressed her fingers at her temples again. "It's the 'or most of it' I think we might have a problem explaining."

"I wouldn't worry about it, El. Your brother knows me well enough to know I'm not the kind of guy to take advantage of a vulnerable woman."

No matter how much he might have wanted to. Okay, as much as he *still* wanted to.

Much to her relief, Matt was right. Grant hadn't kicked up any kind of fuss about her rolling in just after sunrise from a night on the town.

Her brother had just been leaving the house when they pulled up. He didn't say so but Elise suspected he'd been on his way to look for her since he generally didn't go to work at the resort this early in the morning.

She had feared some sort of scene. Grant could have a temper and was the only male she knew more overprotective than Matt. But Grant—the closest thing she had to a father figure since John Clifton's murder a dozen years ago—had given Matt one long, searching look, then apparently accepted the story.

"I really appreciate you keeping her safe," Grant said, clapping Matt on the shoulder. "Somebody without your scruples might have taken advantage of the situation."

Elise remembered that searing kiss and her intense reaction to it. She could feel a blasted blush creep up her cheeks and had to hope Grant didn't notice.

"Glad I could be there. We left her car at The Hitching Post. Need me to shuttle it home for you?"

"No. I can have somebody from the resort drive it out here later this morning."

Elise felt supremely stupid and about ten years old again. She was grateful when Matt said goodbye quickly and left, saying he needed to get to the McFarlane job site early that morning.

After the door closed behind him, she was faced with her headache and Grant, who watched her with a concerned frown.

"I don't get it. After Haley pulled out of your plans, why didn't you just come home and have dinner with us?" he asked. "Erin was sorry she missed you."

She didn't want to sound whiny or self-pitying, especially not when Grant and Helen were so happy about finding Erin. "I was already at The Hitching Post and you all weren't expecting me home so I just decided to stay and enjoy the band. In retrospect, maybe not the smartest decision I ever made, but it worked out okay in the end."

"You were lucky," Grant growled.

She sighed. "I know."

"I don't even want to think about what might have

happened to you if Cates hadn't been there," Grant growled.

"If Cates hadn't been where?"

Her mother walked into the kitchen wearing her favorite green bathrobe and Elise mentally groaned. So much for her furtive hope that she might sneak away from Grant's lecture and climb back to bed to nurse her blasted headache before her mother came downstairs. She was in for it now.

"Elise had a little run-in with a drunk cowboy last night down at The Hitching Post. Matt Cates came to her rescue. That's why she's just rolling in at 6:00 a.m."

"What a nice boy. Those Cates brothers are always so thoughtful." Helen smiled. "They must take after their father. He's always been the nicest man."

Her mother tended only to see the good in people. Either that or she hadn't paid any attention to the Cates twins' antics over the years. Matt and his brother had been wild hell-raisers until recently.

They hadn't completely worked all the wildness out of their systems. She remembered the fierce way Matt had taken on Jake Halloran to protect her and then the stormy, wondrous heat of his kiss.

"Tell me again how you ended up spending the night at Cates's place instead of coming back here after you left The Hitching Post?" Grant asked pointedly, which she found the height of hypocrisy coming from a man who'd enjoyed a healthy reputation as a ladies' man before his surprise marriage to Stephanie three years earlier.

To her surprise and relief, her mother stepped. "I

think that's really Elise's business, don't you?" Helen said with a reassuring pat to Grant's arm.

"I fell asleep on his couch. Relax, Grant. You can put your mind at ease. Matt was a perfect gentleman," she answered. Mostly.

"I would think a perfect gentleman would have made sure you spent the night safe and sound in your own bed."

"I'm here now. Look, don't blame Matt for any of this." Her head hurt and she was embarrassed and wanted nothing more than to crawl into bed and sleep the rest of the morning away but she had to set the record straight first.

"It's all completely my fault. The truth is, I'm embarrassed to admit I wasn't paying attention to my drink quota and I had a little too much on an empty stomach. You know I don't have much tolerance for alcohol."

Last night had truly been full of anomalies and she would be wise to remember that. She rarely drank more than a glass of wine with dinner and the kisses she'd shared with Matt had been a fluke, something that wouldn't happen again.

"Where does the drunk cowboy come in?" her mother asked.

Elise sighed. Maybe they ought to go wake up Steph so she didn't have to go through the story again. "I struck up a conversation at the bar with a Lazy D ranch hand. He mistook our conversation for more of a flirtation than I intended and he…didn't take my attempt at brushing him off with very good grace. He tried to…to kiss me and didn't seem to believe my no really meant no."

"You could have been in serious trouble."

"I know. Believe me, I know." She shivered, remembering again that moment of fear when she had felt overpowered and helpless. "But Matt saw I was having trouble and he stepped in before anything could happen. The two of them got into it a little bit, mostly shoving, pushing, that sort of thing. When it was over, Matt took me back to his place so I could help him clean up and to grab a bite to eat. I'm afraid we both fell asleep. And here we are."

She was leaving out a few details, like how she had cried all over him and then kissed him until she couldn't think straight.

Some things were no one else's business but hers and Matt's.

"I guess I owe the man for looking out for you," Grant said.

"You don't owe him anything. I do."

"Well, you're home now and that's the important thing." Helen pulled her into a hug and Elise held on, closing her eyes and inhaling the clean, wholesome scent of lilacs and Tide detergent that clung to her mother.

Tears stung her eyes and not just from the headache pulsing through her veins. This was the scent of her childhood, when she had felt warm and safe and beloved.

Before she knew anything about wicked people who could kill men because of greed, or innocent hospital mistakes that would come back years later to destroy everything she thought she knew.

"I wish you had stayed," Helen said. "We had a

perfectly lovely evening with Erin. Corey Traub came with her. They make such a wonderful couple."

Elise forced a smile and eased away from her mother. "They seem great together."

"She was sorry to miss you, too. I think she's looking forward to having a sister after growing up only with brothers."

But they weren't sisters. They weren't related at all except for the weird, sadistic twist of fate that had brought them all together.

Elise decided she must be a terrible person. Erin obviously wanted to be friends and Elise couldn't seem to put any effort forward in that direction.

She should have stayed home and tried last night, she thought again. A few hours of being polite seemed a small enough price compared to her humiliation at causing a scene at The Hitching Post and, worse, spilling her angst all over Matt Cates and then sharing a kiss with him.

Her mind replayed those stunning moments at his house—his mouth warm and sexy against hers, the strength of his arms around her, the safety and security she felt near him. The man could definitely kiss. She'd always suspected it and now she knew without a doubt all the whisperings she'd heard around town were based on fact.

For a few moments there, she hadn't been able to think about anything but his touch. Not hospital mistakes or drunk cowboys or even her own name—Elise Clifton or Elise Castro or whoever the heck she was this week.

Chapter Five

"Nice bit of color you've got there, son. Thought I taught you how to duck a little better than that."

Matt made at face at his father, who leaned on the doorjamb of the bedroom at the McFarlane Lodge where they were putting up the last bit of finish trim around the windows and doors.

A guy got in one lousy fight and the whole town wanted to talk about it. He supposed it didn't help when he sported the worst shiner he'd had since he was fourteen, when he and Marlon had gotten a little too physical over a cute cheerleader from Bozeman.

He'd never realized he had a long and painful history of fighting over women.

"Heard you got into it with a drunk cowboy over a girl down at The Hitching Post," piped in Bud Larsen, one of their workers, as he carried in another load of trim from the truck.

Matt used the fine-planed black walnut he was measuring as an excuse to avoid the gaze of either Bud or his father.

"Something like that," he answered evasively.

"Was Christine involved?" Frank asked.

He supposed he couldn't blame his father for jumping to that conclusion. His parents thought he and Christine Mayhew were serious since they had been "dating" steadily for the last few months.

"She wasn't even there, Dad. She had a baby shower last night so I went to hang out with some of the guys."

Frank set the level on the trim to double and triple check, as he always did. "She know you got into a fight over another girl?"

His parents liked Christine. Now that both of his older brothers were married and Marlon was engaged to Haley Anderson, Matt often found himself the object of much teasing and speculation from his family about when he planned to take his turn on that particular merry-go-round.

He had tried to be evasive to his family about his and Christine's relationship but it was becoming more difficult without blatant prevarication, something he tried not to do to his parents very often since they always seemed to catch him at it anyway.

"I don't know if Christine has heard or not. I haven't had a chance to talk to her, but you know how the grapevine works around here."

"Women like to hear those sorts of things straight from the horse, if you get me," Bud offered with a wink.

"I'll keep that in mind," Matt said. He decided he didn't need to mention that he wasn't about to take relationship advice from a man who had been married four times, two of them to sisters.

"Anyway, it was just a misunderstanding."

"So if the girl you tussled over down at the bar wasn't Christine, who the heck was it?" Frank asked.

For some reason, Matt found himself strangely reluctant to tell his father the truth. He knew this was just what Elise had feared, that she would find herself the subject of gossip and speculation.

But he also knew that look in his father's eyes. Frank wouldn't stop until he'd extracted every ounce of available information out of Matt. Sometimes he wondered if his father had undergone interrogation training somewhere in his distant past or if he was just particularly gifted at squeezing information out of his reticent sons.

He should probably just blurt it out, rather than hem and haw and obfuscate, when Frank would just find out sooner or later.

He sighed. "Grant Clifton's sister."

"Elise?" His father registered a moment of surprise then he shook his head. "That poor little thing. She's had a rough time of it this last month, hasn't she?"

"She has."

"If some no-account cowboy was messing with her, you did the right thing, son. She all right?"

He thought of her sobbing out her confusion and pain in his arms and then the stunning, unforgettable kiss that never should have happened. "I think so."

"She's tough, our little Elise."

"Not so little anymore, Dad. We're the same age."

His father again looked surprised. "I guess you are at that. I always forget you went to school with her. Well, I'm glad you were there to watch out for her. Christine will probably understand."

"If she don't and throws you out on your butt, you mind if I have a go?" Bud asked eagerly. "That is one fine-looking woman."

The man was twenty years older than Christine. Hell, he had kids who were older than she was. Matt was trying to come up with a diplomatic response but his father didn't bother.

"Shut up, Bud, and get back to work now before I throw *you* out on your butt," Frank growled.

Bud grumbled but headed back out for another load.

When the other man left, Frank turned to him, his brown eyes uncharacteristically serious. "As much as I hate to say it, I think Bud's probably right about this, anyway. You might want to get out in front of the story. Call Christine and explain your side of the story before she hears a rumor and gets the wrong idea. Be careful there, son. She's a nice girl. You don't want to hurt her."

An image of Elise in his arms flashed through his mind again, a picture he hadn't been able to shake all morning. He didn't worry about hurting Christine. They were only friends. Elise was an entirely different story. "Yeah. I know."

His phone rang just a few moments after his father left to direct the other workers, leaving Matt alone with the work and his thoughts.

Matt pulled it from the holder on his belt and glanced at the caller ID.

"Hey, Christine," he said. "I was just talking about you."

"You're a busy guy, Matt. Rumor has it you pulled the white-knight act last night at The Hitching Post."

How the heck did rumors manage to fly so fast and furiously in a small town? "A guy might think nothing exciting ever happens in Thunder Canyon," he complained. "Doesn't anybody in town have something more interesting to talk about?"

She gave that rich, husky laugh he had always enjoyed. "I guess tongues all over town are going to wag when one of the supposedly reformed hell-raising Cates boys comes out of retirement."

"Yeah, yeah."

She laughed again. "That's why I'm calling, actually. I'm just wondering if you want to cancel our plans for tonight."

"Why would I do that?"

"I just figured, now that you've apparently taken on the cause of some other damsel in distress, you might be too busy."

Elise might have returned his kiss the night before with a sweet passion, but for all he knew, that might have only been the margaritas talking. "I'm never too busy for you, Chris. As far as I'm concerned, we're still on."

"And the bar fight I'm hearing about? From what I understand, you whomped on a Lazy D cowboy."

"All a misunderstanding," he repeated what he'd told his father.

"And the girl?"

"Elise is just an old friend," he lied. "I'm definitely looking forward to dinner."

"So am I. I owe you. Taking you to The Gallatin Room is the least I can do to repay you for helping me out these last few months."

"How many times will I have to remind you I was happy to be able to help, before you start to believe me?"

"A few more, maybe."

He smiled. "It's been fun, Christine. And I think your devious plot worked. You haven't been bothered by Clay for a while, have you?"

"Not much. The stray email here and there and message on voice mail but I can always delete those."

"So does seven tomorrow still work?" he asked.

"Perfectly. Try not to get into any more barfights between now and then. I might have a tough time explaining why my supposed boyfriend is ripping it up down at The Hitching Post over another woman."

"Maybe because you won't give it up," he teased.

She laughed hard. "Ewww. Don't even go there, Matt. Don't get me wrong, you're gorgeous and all, but it's like kissing a brother."

He couldn't fault her for that since he'd had a very similar reaction.

"Sorry, I've got to run," she said a few moments later. "This place is crazy with Christmas shoppers today. I'll see you tonight, okay?"

After he hung up, he paused for a moment, gazing out the window at the spectacular view of the mountains from the McFarlane Lodge. Some part of him really wished he could stir up something more than friendship with Christine. She was perfect for him in many ways. Fun and exuberant and undeniably beautiful.

A few months ago, he never would have believed it, but he was beginning to feel ready to start thinking about the next phase of his life. Maybe it was Marlon's relationship with Haley that had set him on the road, but his life had begun to seem empty.

He loved the job. He loved the challenge of rehabbing houses on the side. He enjoyed hanging with the guys and going fly-fishing and watching basketball games. But something had been missing for a while.

His thoughts filled with Elise again—the softness of her mouth, the startling hunger racing through him, that incredible wash of tenderness as he held her while she slept.

He had a fierce desire to see where things might take them but it was tempered by the awareness that this was abysmal timing for her. She was dealing with a lot right now, stresses he couldn't begin to imagine. Maybe what she needed most from him was a little patience, something that had never been one of his strengths.

He sighed. He wasn't going to get this project finished

in time for Connor McFarlane's grand lodge opening if he didn't focus.

He had to stop thinking about Elise. A pleasant evening with Christine would be the perfect diversion.

He hoped.

"We'll have your table ready in just a moment, Mr. Clifton."

"No problem, Sara. We don't mind waiting."

Elise felt a pang of sympathy for the hostess at The Gallatin Room at the Thunder Canyon Resort, who looked on the verge of a full-fledged panic attack that her boss and his family had to wait even thirty seconds.

Grant had been running the ski resort—now a four-season destination—for several years. He seemed to be highly respected by his employees, with perhaps a healthy amount of fear added to the mix.

She had a hard time reconciling his professional persona with her teasing, sometimes annoying older brother.

After her disaster of an outing the night before at The Hitching Post and the gossip she knew likely had galloped through town, her first instinct was to stay at the ranch where she was safe, to avoid showing her face around town. But her usually sweet mother could be stubborn about certain things.

"We've hardly had a moment with Grant and Stephanie since…well, since everything happened with Erin and since you and I came back to Thunder Canyon," Helen had said that afternoon. "With Grant's busy schedule from now until New Year's, who knows when we'll have time for a family dinner again."

Elise hadn't known how to wiggle out of it. As the hostess finally led them through the always-crowded restaurant toward the best table overlooking the snow-covered mountains, she wished she'd tried a little harder.

Many of the guests were tourists in town for holiday skiing but she recognized several locals, who all seemed to follow the Cliftons' progress through the restaurant with avid, hungry gazes.

"I hate this," she muttered under her breath.

She really hadn't meant to say the words aloud but she must have. Stephanie, Grant's wife, tucked her arm through Elise's. "Hate what, honey?"

"Everybody's staring and whispering at us," she finally said. "I feel like some kind of circus freak."

Stephanie's blue eyes warmed with compassion and she smiled, squeezing Elise's arm. "And here I thought they were staring at me, in all my voluptuous glory."

Elise had to laugh. Steph was seven months pregnant, due in February, but carried the baby well on her slim, athletic frame.

"You're right." Elise smiled back, grateful at Steph for yanking her out of her pity party. "What else would they be looking at but how utterly, gorgeously pregnant you are? How narcissistic of me to automatically assume I'm always the center of attention."

"Wait until you're either a bride or pregnant for that," Steph said.

By then they had reached their table and Grant pulled

out the chairs for all three of the women. "Aren't I the luckiest guy here, to have the three most beautiful women in town at my table?"

"Suck-up," Elise muttered, earning a grin from her older brother. She couldn't resist returning his smile. Elise reached for her water glass when the hostess filled it, then nearly dumped the whole thing over when she spotted the couple sitting only three tables away from them.

Matt Cates seemed to be enjoying a very cozy dinner for two with a slender, lovely brunette. The woman was laughing at something he said and leaning into him, her body language clearly telegraphing an easy, comfortable familiarity. While they spoke, the woman kept one hand on his arm as if she didn't want to let him go—the same arm that the night before had pulled Elise to him and held her close while she slept.

She told herself to look away. His choice in dinner companions was absolutely none of her business, and she would do well to remember that. She was not about to spend the evening gawking at him.

She had just started to heed her own advice and shift her attention back to her family when he suddenly happened to look straight at her. Rats. Caught. Just like in junior high when she used to moon over him in Mrs. McLarty's algebra class.

Something flashed in his eyes as he smiled at her. She jerked her gaze away, fumbling with her flatware and knocking her salad fork into her lap.

"Everything okay?" Stephanie asked in an undertone.

"Sure. Fine. Just great. Why wouldn't it be?"

She let out a breath. Naturally, she had a clear view of the two of them from her vantage point. If she didn't suspect it would spark a host of questions she wasn't in the mood to answer, Elise would have asked her mother to switch places so she didn't have to sit and watch him. Instead, she would just have to force herself not to stare.

There were plenty of other restaurants in town. Why did they both have to choose tonight to come to this particular one? she wondered. His presence—complete with that spectacular black eye—was certain to generate plenty more conversation among anyone who might have heard even a whisper of a rumor about the altercation the night before.

Grant spied him at the same moment and lifted a hand. Matt returned the greeting before turning back to his companion.

"His shiner's looking even prettier," Grant said just as their waiter approached with an obsequious smile.

Grant cut him off at the pass before he could even go into his spiel welcoming them to The Gallatin Room.

"Listen, Marcos. I need you to do me a favor."

"Of course, Mr. Clifton. Anything."

"Send a bottle of our best Cabernet Sauvignon to table seventeen, with my compliments," he answered.

Curiosity flashed briefly in the man's eyes but he quickly concealed it and nodded. "Of course, sir. Right away, sir."

He hurried away and Elise rolled her eyes at her

brother with an exasperated sigh. "Was that really necessary?"

Grant smiled. "He protected my baby sister from a sticky situation and has the battle scars to prove it. I'd say it is."

Would Grant be so amused by the whole thing if he knew about the heated kiss she and Matt had shared?

Elise snapped her napkin out onto her lap, trying not to remember the heat of his mouth and the strength of his arms and the liquid pool of desire seeping through her.

A moment later, the sommelier delivered a bottle to Matt's table. He acknowledged Grant's gift with a wry smile to her brother, which Elise pretended not to notice.

The next hour was a definite challenge. Through each course, she had to work hard not to gawk at Matt and his companion. She made a pointed effort to enjoy the delicious dinner, though each bite seemed a chore.

Halfway through the main course, she excused herself to use the restroom, located just outside the restaurant in the main lobby area. When she emerged, she was somehow not surprised to find Matt waiting for her.

He looked far more delicious than the roasted chicken and new potatoes she had ordered, in a cream-colored sweater that made him look dark and gorgeous in contrast.

"How's the head?" he asked.

She made a face. "Better. Just be glad you didn't ask me that a few hours ago or you would have a headache of your own after I bit yours off."

He smiled. "I'm glad you're feeling better."

Why did he make her feel so safe and warm just inhabiting the same air space? It was completely ridiculous, this yearning of hers to stand here and bask in his smile.

She suddenly remembered his companion. "Your date is lovely," she said, working hard to ignore the sinking sensation in the pit of her stomach, that pinch of jealousy she had no right to feel.

For an instant, he looked slightly taken aback, as if he'd forgotten all about the poor woman, then he nodded. "Do you know Christine Mayhew?"

"I'm not sure we've met."

They lapsed into awkward silence. She was just about to excuse herself when he gestured toward the dining room. "You look as if you're enjoying your dinner. How are things with your family? Better?"

She fidgeted, embarrassed at the reminder of her emotional breakdown at his house. "Yes. Fine."

"I've been worried about you today."

Her cheeks felt hot and she cursed her fair skin that revealed every hint of embarrassment. "Don't. I'm fine, mostly just embarrassed that I fell apart like that. I learned a hard lesson, that too much alcohol turns me into a bawl-baby. You'll notice I'm not having anything stronger than ginger ale tonight. I really am sorry, Matt, for putting you through that and dumping all my troubles on you."

"I'm glad I could be there. If you, you know, need to talk or anything, you know where to find me."

He looked completely sincere and Elise felt a tiny

little tug on her heart. "Thank you. I appreciate that. I think I'm done feeling sorry for myself for a while. I've even got a job. Well, sort of. Haley called and asked me to help her with the ROOTS Christmas party next week. Staying busy will help."

"Good. That's great. I'll be there, too. Marlon has demanded—I mean, asked me in no uncertain terms—that I help out at the party."

Apparently she wouldn't be able to completely avoid him during the rest of her stay. She didn't know whether to rejoice or be depressed by that.

Elise glanced inside the dining room where the rest of her family members looked to be finishing up their meal. Stephanie was already gesturing for Marcos to take away her plate. "I should go. And you probably need to return to your date."

"Right."

He followed her gaze to the other diners, then shifted his attention back to her. He seemed strangely reluctant to leave her company, but she must be misinterpreting things. He was here with a date. A beautiful, vivacious date. Why would he want to hang around in a hallway with her when he could be sitting out there with a pretty brunette? She knew the thought shouldn't depress her so much.

"I guess I'll see you around ROOTS, then," he said.

"Enjoy your evening," she answered, then hurried back inside the restaurant to rejoin her family, trying hard not to wish *she* were the one sharing that bottle of wine with him.

* * *

"So that's Elise."

Matt returned his napkin to his lap, careful not to meet Christine's gaze. She was entirely too perceptive. For some reason, he was hesitant to let her see the depth of his attraction for Elise. Even though he and Christine were strictly friends, showing such blatant interest in another woman seemed rude.

"Yes. Grant's little sister."

"But she's not really, right? Grant's sister, I mean. She's the one who was switched at birth with Erin Castro."

"That doesn't make her any less Grant's sister," he answered, more curtly than he intended. He couldn't shake the memory of her anguish the night before as she had sobbed out her confusion in his arms.

Christine raised an eyebrow but said nothing and he squirmed. Yeah. Entirely too perceptive. So much for concealing his growing feelings for Elise.

"She's very pretty," Christine said after a moment. "Has she moved back to Thunder Canyon for good?"

He was wondering that same thing. "Not sure yet."

She was quiet for a moment then she touched his forearm. "Whenever you want to stage a breakup, you only have to say the word. You've been wonderful these last few months but this arrangement of ours was never supposed to be open-ended."

"Why do we need to change anything?"

She smiled. "I don't know. Maybe because you haven't stopped sneaking glances over at the Clifton table all night."

He took a sip of the delicious wine Grant had sent over to thank him for doing what any decent man would do. "I'm sorry," he murmured.

"Why are you sorry? This isn't a real date, Matt. You're not breaking any unwritten rules here. I'm just saying, I'll step out of the picture whenever you want me to."

He mulled her offer, not sure exactly how to respond. How was it possible that one crazy evening with Elise seemed to have changed everything?

"What about Clay?"

Christine shrugged. "I'll deal. If he hasn't gotten the message by now that I've moved on, the man needs serious help. I don't know what more I can do."

He had thought more than once that Christine was too softhearted. From the moment she broke up with Clay Robbins, she should have been clear that she was breaking up with him because he was clingy and obsessive. Instead, she had tried to let him down gently. When that didn't work, she had enlisted Matt's help to convince the other man she had moved on.

In Matt's opinion, the man needed somebody to knock him ass over teakettle until he clued in that Christine wasn't interested. Sort of like Jake Halloran the night before at The Hitching Post.

They finished their dinner not long after that. A surreptitious peek at the Cliftons' table while he was waiting for their server to return the check revealed they were lingering over dessert. He supposed it would be better to leave before they finished to avoid any awkwardness with Elise or the embarrassment of having to endure more unwanted gratitude from her family over the events of the night before.

He and Christine walked out into the lobby of the resort, with its leather sofas and life-size elk sculpture. He grabbed her coat and was helping her into it when her shoulders suddenly tensed beneath his hands and she inhaled sharply.

"Sorry. Did I pull your hair?" he asked, feeling big and fumbling.

"No," she whispered with a panicked look at a group that had just entered the lobby carrying holiday presents, obviously out for a night of festive celebrating.

"That's Kelly Robbins, Clay's cousin."

"Which one?"

"The one in the plaid sweater."

He saw exactly when the thin-as-a-rail other woman recognized Christine. Her eyes widened and jumped between the two of them, resting on his hands still at Christine's shoulders as he finished helping her with her coat.

"She's the biggest gossip in the whole blasted county."

"Is that right?" Some spark of recklessness must still be lingering in him from the tussle the night before at The Hitching Post. Heedless of the consequences, he threw an arm over Christine's shoulders.

"She's coming this way," he muttered. "Smile. It's about damn time Clay got the message once and for all."

"What are you going to do?"

"Just play along," he said. "Let's go say hello."

"Matt…" Christine said in a warning tone, but before she could finish, Matt dragged her over to the group of chattering women, who happened conveniently to be located near the entrance to the valet parking, anyway.

Christine gave a polished sort of smile. "Hi, Kelly. I thought that was you."

The other woman gave a high-pitched squeal, just as if she hadn't already seen them five minutes earlier. He could already tell she was exactly the sort of woman who always grated on his nerves, plastic and gushy.

"Christine! Hi! You look *gorgeous!* I haven't seen you in *ages!* Not since you and Clay…well, not in *forever.* How are you?"

Christine sent him a help-me sort of sidelong look as if she were waiting for his grand master plan.

"Good. Great. Um, Kelly Robbins, this is Matt Cates. Matt, Kelly lives over in Bozeman. I used to…um, date her cousin."

"You're Clay Robbins's cousin?" he asked, forcing a note of intrigue in his voice.

"Yes," she said slowly with a wary sort of look.

"How is Clay these days?" Matt asked. "I guess I should feel sorry for the poor guy but I just can't."

He squeezed Christine's shoulders, laying the cheese on as thick as he dared.

"Why is that?" the other woman asked, her over-bright friendliness beginning to show a few hairline fractures.

"He really did me a favor, breaking up with Christine. If things had worked out with the two of them, I wouldn't be about to become the luckiest guy in the world."

He kissed her temple, lingering there with his mouth in her hair as if he couldn't bear to lose contact with her, in exactly the sort of public display of affection that always gave him the creeps.

He was probably going overboard here. Christine obviously thought so, at least judging by the heel of her boot that was currently digging into his instep.

"You're getting married?" Kelly squealed. She yanked Christine out of his arms and pulled her into a hug and even from here he could smell the spicy holiday-scented perfume she must have spritzed heavily before walking out the door. "When is the big day?"

Christine slanted him a sour look over the other woman's shoulder and Matt grinned back at her.

He tried to dissemble as much as he could manage to get away with. "You know how it is. Nothing's official yet. We're, uh, still working out the details. Keep it to yourself though, okay?"

Kelly gushed for a moment or two more. "I'm happy for you. Really I am." She frowned as if she'd suddenly thought of something, when Matt knew damn well she'd only been trying to figure out a way to work it into the conversation. "It's just, well, Clay's gonna be pretty upset, you know."

Christine sighed and then sent Matt a swift look. "I'm sorry for that but I guess it's time he moved on and found someone else, like I have."

"I s'pose," she said.

She looked as if she might say more but the hostess

at that moment came out from The Gallatin Room to let her party know their tables were ready.

"Congratulations again," Kelly said. "Let me know when the big day is, won't you?"

"Nothing's official," Christine protested, with another sideways glare at him.

"That ought to do it," he said, dropping his arm as soon as Kelly was out of view inside the restaurant. "If Robbins doesn't get the message after that, he's more of an idiot than I thought."

Christine somehow managed to look relieved and upset at the same time. "You're crazy, do you know that?" she said, shaking her head. "What are you going to do when the rumor starts flying around Thunder Canyon that we're engaged?"

"Who's going to talk? I didn't recognize a single one of those ladies and I know everybody in town. They must be from Bozeman. Who are they going to tell?"

"Don't you think Clay will figure out something's hinky when this engagement of ours never materializes?"

"Who knows?" Matt shrugged. "By then, he'll hopefully have found some other poor woman to cling to."

She was quiet for a moment as they walked out of the lodge and into the December night, starry and cold and lit by little twinkling gold lights adorning the lodge.

"What about Elise Clifton?" she asked as they waited for the valet to bring his pickup. "What if she hears rumors we're engaged?"

"There's nothing going on between Elise and me," he said, even though the words weren't precisely true.

What would it matter if she did find out? She probably wouldn't care, even if it were true. Elise was a friend—that was all.

Yet he was suddenly shocked to find himself wanting much more.

Chapter Six

"You need to march straight home and climb back to bed, missy. I'm not going to listen to any more arguments."

Elise stared down at Haley. Her best friend, who was currently huddled at her desk at ROOTS with a blanket over her shoulders, a nearly empty box of tissues at her elbow and complete misery on her features.

"I can't be sick another minute. I have way too much to do!" Haley wailed, then gave a wretched-sounding cough. "The Christmas party is only four days away and I still have to finish the decorations and make sure the caterers are ready and organize the swag bags from all the donations we've received."

"And if you don't get some rest and take care of yourself, you're going to be in a hospital bed while the rest of us throw a party. Go home, Hale."

"I can't just dump it all on you."

"I don't mind. Knowing you, I imagine your notes are extensive enough that I can figure out everything."

"It still doesn't seem right."

Elise wasn't always the most firm person on the planet, but she wasn't going to budge about this. "Go home," she repeated. "If not for your own sake, think about all these kids you love so much. What if you pass on all your pesky little germs and make them sick for the holidays?"

Haley opened her mouth to answer, then closed it again and slumped a little further down in her chair. "You're right. Darn it, you're right."

"Of course I am. Come on, I'll help you to your car."

Haley sighed heavily as if the very idea of moving just then was far beyond her capabilities. She lifted her hands to the arms of her desk chair but before she could rise, the door to ROOTS opened with a blast of cold air.

For a moment, Elise felt her heartbeat skitter at the tall, muscled figure who walked through, then she shook herself. Not Matt. Despite the fact that he shared the same brown hair and eyes and those sturdy, cry-on-me shoulders, this was Marlon, Matt's twin brother. She could tell in an instant, though she wasn't exactly certain how she knew.

He stood inside the renovated storefront that now housed Haley's volunteer organization aimed at helping

Thunder Canyon's troubled youth. Marlon looked between the two of them. "What's going on?"

"I'm trying to convince your stubborn girlfriend that she needs to be home in bed."

He raised his eyebrows. "Funny, that's exactly what I told her when she managed to crawl out this morning."

"It's just a cold," Haley insisted, though her brown eyes were bloodshot, her nose red, her skin pale. "I'll be fine."

"Sure you will." Elise said briskly. "You'll be good as new in a day or two. In the meantime, I can handle things here. I don't want you to worry for a single moment. I think I can manage to answer phones and make some Christmas decorations without ROOTS falling completely apart."

"It's such a lousy time to be sick. I have so much to *do.*"

Elise shared a sympathetic look with Marlon and was struck again by the similarities yet differences between him and Matt.

"Nothing that's so important it's worth jeopardizing your health to accomplish," Marlon said sternly. "Come on, I'll drop you back at home and tuck you in with a cup of tea and a good book."

Was she a terrible person that she actually envied her friend? Oh, not for the lousy cold. She would happily leave that to Haley since Elise hated being sick worse than just about anything. But Marlon's tender concern for the woman he loved touched a chord somewhere deep inside, left her with a nameless ache in her chest.

Though she dated here and there, she had avoided any serious entanglements the last few years after a nasty experience with her ex-boyfriend. As she watched Haley and Marlon together, Elise had to wonder if she'd been wrong. A broken heart—or more accurately, probably, bruised ego—from one cheating louse didn't mean she had to give up all hope of finding what Haley and Marlon shared.

"Go home and go back to bed," Elise said again. "When you wake up later today, you can email me your to-do list. Meantime, I can start with the Christmas decorations for the party."

"Are you sure?"

"Positive. Go home. If you don't go on your own, I have a feeling Marlon over there will toss you over his shoulder and haul you out of here."

"Really?" Haley shifted her gaze to the man. For the first time since Elise had walked into ROOTS a half hour ago, she saw a tiny smile on her friend's face.

Marlon grinned. "In a heartbeat, sweetheart. Want to try me? Come on, let's get you home."

Though Haley still looked far from convinced, Elise and Marlon finally managed to usher her out the door and into Marlon's vehicle.

After they left, Elise turned around to survey this place her friend loved so much. The place wasn't fancy but Haley had managed to turn it into a comfortable hangout for troubled local teens. The wall facing the street was covered in a mural that Haley painted—kids with books, computers, sports images. A couch covered with a slipcover took up one wall and in a corner was a TV with video games.

Haley loved it here and was passionate about helping her teens. Elise knew Haley came up with the idea after her own brother Austin ran into trouble and was helped through it by some local ranching folk. Haley had more than paid it forward by providing a foundation for kids who might be feeling similarly rootless.

Elise envied Haley her dedication and determination. She wasn't sure she had ever cared as passionately for anything.

Oh, she had worked hard to earn her bachelor's degree in business and had enjoyed her job managing a bookstore in Billings. She wanted to think she had been good at her job—good enough that her district manager had assured her he would only accept a temporary leave of absence rather than a full-on resignation when she made the decision to come to Thunder Canyon for the holidays after Erin's stunning revelation.

While she had enjoyed the challenges of running a small bookstore, she couldn't say she really missed it. What she *had* missed was the chance to do something constructive. The last two weeks, she had tried to stay busy by helping out at the ranch but Stephanie had everything running so smoothly there, Elise had mostly been in the way.

She actually relished the chance to help Haley out at ROOTS for a few days, if only to provide a distraction from everything that had happened in the last month.

If the work also helped divert her mind from Marlon's gorgeous twin brother, she considered that a definite bonus.

* * *

Several hours later, Elsie was questioning her sanity. Her fingers had a dozen pinpricks from stringing popcorn and cranberries for the tree garlands, her neck had cramped about an hour ago and her eyes were blurry and achy from concentrating.

Added to that, all afternoon, ROOTS had been a madhouse with people coming in and out to make deliveries of donations for the party and the phone had been ringing off the hook with people asking questions she couldn't answer.

Since the high school let out, a couple dozen teens had descended to do homework or play video games or just to hang out.

Now, near 6:00 p.m., they had all dispersed, leaving her alone again to finish up the Christmas decorations.

Night came early at this latitude as Montana was headed for the shortest day of the year in a week, and outside the Christmas lights up and down the streets of Old Town Thunder Canyon had slowly flickered on.

There. One more cranberry and she was calling this one good. She tied the knot on the string then carried the garland to the back room to go with the rest of the decorations, twisting her neck from side to side as she walked, to stretch her achy muscles. She laid it carefully across the folding table she had unearthed from a corner and had set up to hold the decorations. She flipped off the light to return to the front when she suddenly heard the jingling bells on the door.

So much for locking up. Who would be coming this

late? Probably somebody with another donation. The generosity of the townspeople had been a definite eye-opener.

Elise gave a weary sigh and headed out to greet the newcomer.

As soon as she spied the tall, dark-haired man near the door, her heart gave a ridiculous little leap and this time she didn't even wonder for an instant which Cates brother it was.

"Matt. Hi!"

He entered the room with that long-legged, loose-hipped walk of his and her stomach sizzled.

Surprise and something else—something that left her hot and edgy—flashed in his eyes. "Oh! You're not Haley."

"No. She's a few inches taller and her hair is brown and quite a bit longer. And you're not Marlon."

He sent her a sidelong look and she saw the teasing sparkle in his eyes. The Cates boys had been notorious in school for playing tricks on people, pretending to be each other at the most inconvenient moments.

"You sure about that?" he asked.

She stacked stray papers on Haley's desk so her workspace would be neat in the morning. "Completely. Marlon's the good-looking one."

Surprise flickered in those brown eyes again and then he laughed. "Wow. A little harsh, don't you think?"

All the stresses of the day seemed to shimmer away like silvery tinsel on the wind. How did he have that effect on her? she wondered. She had no idea—but she was very much afraid she might become addicted to it.

"You know I'm joking. You're identical twins, both of you too gorgeous for your own good."

As soon as the words were out, she couldn't believe she had actually spoken them aloud. She wasn't exactly the flirty, lighthearted type. Actually, she had always been a little on the shy side when it came to men, especially big, sexy men like Matt Cates.

He didn't seem to find her remark out of character but it did seem to make him uncomfortable. He rolled his eyes and she thought she detected a slight hint of color on his features. Really? Could he honestly not be aware of his effect on the opposite sex? He had been breaking girls' hearts since grade school.

"Seriously, how can you tell?" he asked her with a quizzical look. "Sometimes our own parents aren't sure."

"Besides the black eye, you mean? I'm not quite sure. I just know." She studied him, trying to figure out the signs she took for granted. "Your chins are shaped a little differently, I guess. Your hair's just a little more streaky than his. Oh, and your lashes are just a bit longer."

He still looked baffled and Elise could feel herself blush. How could she tell him she had spent a long time staring at him when he wasn't paying her any attention, from the time she was old enough to even notice him?

"However you do it, it's amazing. Not many people can tell us apart." He looked around. "So is Haley here?"

"No. Your brother—"

"You mean the good-looking one?" he interrupted. She smiled. "Right. Marlon took her home earlier.

She's got a bad cold and is feeling lousy. She tried to tough it out here at ROOTS for a while but seemed to be getting worse, not better. I offered to step in to help her with the Christmas party Friday so she could recover and keep her bad juju to herself."

"Oh, right. I forgot about the party."

She pointed to the boxes of donations. "If you'd like, I've got about a hundred gift bags to fill that might jog your memory."

"Tonight?"

He sounded as if he was completely willing to sit right down and start throwing bags together, which she found rather wonderful.

"No. I'll probably work on them a little later in the week once all the donations come in. But thanks for the offer. Haley might take you up on it if she comes back in time to crack the whip over all the volunteers." She paused. "Sorry, you must have had a reason for coming in to see Haley. Is there something I can help you with?"

He didn't say anything for several beats, only looked at her with that glittery look in his eyes again, until her skin felt achy and tight.

After a moment, he cleared his throat. "Actually, I had a good excuse to come visit Haley but that's all it was. An excuse. In reality, I was trying to be sneaky."

"You? Sneaky? Imagine that!"

He ignored her dry tone. "You know, finding you here instead of Haley works out even better for me. You're the perfect person to help me out."

"Am I?"

He sat on the edge of the desk and she tried not to feel overwhelmed by all that rugged strength so close to her. "You've been friends with Haley for a long time, right? So you know her pretty well."

"She and Steph have been my closest friends forever."

"Great!" He grinned and she had to remind herself to breathe. "This is perfect. You can come to Bozeman with me tonight."

She blinked. "Excuse me?"

"I'm trying to find a Christmas present for her. Not just any Christmas present, the perfect Christmas present. She's the only one left on my list."

That he had a list in the first place struck her as odd. That he was enlisting her help to cross Haley's name off that list was even more surreal. "She's really the only one whose present you haven't bought yet? You still have another week and a half before Christmas. I thought most guys tended to wait until the last minute."

He manufactured an affronted look. "That is a blatant stereotype, Ms. Clifton, and I am personally offended by it."

She couldn't help herself—she smiled. She couldn't remember the last time she had felt this, well, happy. "Oh, sorry to be a reverse chauvinist. But every man *I* know waits until the last minute. Grant and my cousin Bo are the worst."

He shrugged. "I happen to love Christmas and the whole giving-presents thing. I've had almost everything done and even wrapped for a while now, except for Haley's gift. She's still fairly new to our family circle and since this is her first Christmas with us, I wanted to find something special. I'm heading into Bozeman right now before all the stores close and dropped by ROOTS hoping I could finesse a few hints out of her about what she would like before I leave."

"I'm sorry she's not here."

"Not at all. Now you can come with me, which is even better. I'll even spring for dinner. What time are you closing up shop here?"

"I was just about to. But I can't just…"

"Sure you can," he said over her objections. "Come on, it will be fun."

She could think of a dozen reasons why she shouldn't go with him. She was tired. She had a headache. She wasn't thrilled about her silly, futile crush on him and had been warning herself since Saturday morning when he dropped her off back at Clifton's Pride that she needed to keep her distance so she didn't make an even bigger fool of herself over him.

But her words to Grant that morning after he drove away still echoed in her mind. She owed him for coming to her rescue the other night at The Hitching Post—and he still had the vividly colored eye to show for it.

Without him, she might have found herself in serious trouble with Jake Halloran. He had stepped in to rescue her from a jam at considerable risk to himself. All he wanted now was the simple favor of helping him select a gift. If she went with him to Bozeman, perhaps she wouldn't feel quite so indebted to him.

The trick would be making it through the evening alone with him without completely humiliating herself while the memory of that stunning kiss simmered under her skin.

"Fine." She spoke quickly before she could change her mind. "But since you apparently love Christmas so much, I'm still going to expect you to help me fill those gift bags."

"It's a deal." He grinned and helped her find her coat.

"Are you sure about this?"

Two hours later, they stood inside an art gallery just before closing time looking at an elaborate—and elaborately priced—needlework sampler that depicted an old, gnarled oak tree. In the thin, topmost branches perched a stately, magnificent eagle with its wings outstretched, gleaming gold as if reflecting sunlight.

"Positive. Oh, Matt. It's perfect. Haley will love it."

He studied the piece. It was lovely, in an artsy sort of way. He could see where Haley would probably enjoy it. Elise seemed convinced, anyway. The moment they had walked into the gallery after searching fruitlessly through three or four other crowded stores, she saw it hanging on the wall and gasped with delight.

"You're the expert, I guess," he said now.

"Trust me, she's going to love it. It's perfect," she said again. "So perfect it might have been custom made for her. You know that's the reason she named her teen organization ROOTS, right? Because of a sampler her mother had hanging on the wall. It said something about how there are but two lasting bequests we can give children—roots and wings. This covers both of those things.

I mean it. With this present you're going to win the best future brother-in-law race, hands down."

"Well that's something, at least," he said dryly. "I wouldn't want her favoring Marshall or Mitch over me."

"Haley's going to love it," she assured him. "In fact, she just might wonder if she's marrying the wrong twin."

He made a face as they headed to the salesperson seated behind a discreet counter. "I doubt that. The two of them seem to forget that anybody else on earth even exists when they're together."

He paid for the needlework, gulping a little at the price tag but grateful again that Cates Construction had managed to avoid the worst of the economic downturn so he could splurge a little for his twin's future wife.

"Would you like this gift wrapped?" the saleswoman asked.

"Please. Gift wrapping isn't one of my particular skills."

While the salesclerk carried the piece over to a nearby table where wrapping supplies were neatly organized, Elise picked up their conversation.

"Do you mind? About Marlon and Haley, I mean? The two of you have always been so close. Do you worry she'll interfere with that bond?"

He thought about Haley and the changes she had wrought in his brother. She was sweet and loving, as different as he could imagine from his formerly wild twin. Somehow the two of them managed to still perfectly complement each other.

"Haley's been great for Marlon," he answered honestly. "She centers him, you know? Before she came along, the only thing Marlon really cared about was having a good time and making the next deal. Now he's as passionate about ROOTS as Haley is. They're crazy about each other."

"I noticed." She smiled a little and gave him a considering look. "I guess that leaves you the last Cates standing, which is probably exactly where you want to be, right?"

He gazed at Elise, bright and lovely in the recessed lighting of the gallery. Whenever he looked at her, something soft and tender lodged just under his chest.

Maybe he ought to be a little uneasy about how quickly everything he always thought he wanted had shifted in the last few days, but all he could manage to drum up was gratitude that she had come back to Thunder Canyon.

"I don't expect that particular situation will last long," he said, purposely vague. A guy had to hope, right?

She gave him an uncertain look but he decided not to explain yet. He could be patient, give her time to figure out her feelings.

"Well, whoever manages to capture the last Cates will be a very lucky woman, I'm sure. Especially if you're always so generous with your gifts."

Now would probably be a really good time to change the subject, he decided, before she started to probe too deeply into areas he wasn't quite ready to discuss.

"What about you?" he asked her. "What's on your Christmas list this year?"

She shrugged. "My gifts are already all wrapped this year. When you work in a bookstore, it's easy to find something perfect for everyone on your list."

"I meant for yourself. What are you asking Santa to bring you?"

She looked reluctant to answer and he saw relief in her blue eyes when the saleswoman brought back his wrapped gift for Haley before he could probe a little more.

"Will there be anything else?" the woman asked in the brisk, tired tone of someone who had spent hours on her feet dealing with holiday shoppers.

"Not tonight. But thank you. This is perfect," he said.

He held the door open for Elise and they walked out into the frosty night. A light snow was falling and a few flakes landed on her crimson knit hat and then on her eyelashes.

"You were saying about your Christmas list…" he prompted.

She made a face. "You're about the most persistent man I know."

"I haven't even gotten started yet."

She sighed. "I'm not a big Christmas fan, if you want to know the truth. I haven't been in a long time. Probably since my dad's murder. It's always a difficult time but I'm afraid this year I feel even less like celebrating."

He studied her there in the fluttery snow and that soft tenderness swelled up inside him again. She had certainly been faced with a rough road to walk. He thought of his own family, the parties and traditions and craziness of a Cates family Christmas.

So much had been taken from Elise. He wanted to give her something back but he didn't have the first idea how to help her enjoy Christmas again.

"Come on," he said suddenly. "Let's lock Haley's present in my truck and then take a walk through town before we grab a bite to eat."

She stared at him in the light reflected from the gallery's front window. "Take a walk? It's got to be fifteen degrees out! Are you crazy?"

"Maybe. Probably." He grinned at her. "Come on, let's enjoy some of the Christmas decorations and then I'll buy you dinner at my favorite steak house."

She laughed, though he saw a little lingering sadness in her eyes. "You're in a very strange mood tonight."

"What's strange about being happy? It's Christmas and I'm with the prettiest woman in Bozeman. What guy wouldn't be happy about that?"

Rosy color climbed her cheeks and he knew it wasn't from the cold. Her blushes fascinated and charmed him. On impulse, he pulled her toward him with his free arm for just a moment, leaning in to kiss her forehead. Up close, her eyes were wide and startled and impossibly blue.

He wanted to stay there holding her for a long time while the snow eddied around them and the Christmas lights twinkled in the storefronts, but he sensed she needed a cautious approach.

He eased away and took her hand. "Come on. Let's see if we can find you a little holiday spirit."

They took their time dropping off the package for Haley in his truck then wandering through the streets of Bozeman, listening to the carols playing from speakers out front of the businesses and peering into the all the storefronts like they were children dreaming about the biggest, best bicycle in town.

He found every moment magical, especially watching her eyes lose a little of that lost, haunted look. She laughed and joked with him like the girl he remembered and through the knit of her gloves, her fingers curled inside his as if she didn't want to let go.

By the time they reached his favorite restaurant, his toes were numb from the cold but he wouldn't have changed an instant.

Though the popular steak house could be crowded, business was slow this late on a weeknight and they didn't have to wait long for a table.

She looked lighter somehow, he thought as the hostess seated them and rattled through the evening's specials. Maybe that's what she needed most. Someone to make her smile and help her forget her troubles for a moment.

He wanted to give her the gift of a happy, lighthearted evening where she could forget her worries—and this was definitely one present he didn't need anyone else's help to deliver.

Chapter Seven

How did he do it?

Elise studied the man across the low-lit table from her, strong and dark and gorgeous. Though both Cates twins had been wild, Marlon had always been the charmer while Matt had always seemed more the studious type—one reason he had gravitated toward law school, she supposed.

But tonight, he was making every effort to charm her...and it was definitely working. If she wasn't careful, she would fall hard and fast for him.

She would just have to be careful, she warned herself as her insides trembled from another of his smiles.

"So you never really answered me the other night. How long do you think you're staying in Thunder Canyon?" he asked, in a tone of voice that made her think he had genuine interest in her answer.

She refused to let him fluster her. Matt might be the studious one but he had a reputation as being every bit the player that Marlon used to be.

"I'm not sure," she answered. "I promised my mother I would spend the holidays in town. For now that's what I'm focusing on, just spending time at the ranch and helping Haley at ROOTS while I'm here. Once the holidays are over, I don't know. I'm considering my options."

"What are they? Maybe I can help."

"My job is still waiting for me in Billings if I want it. That's a definite possibility. My life is there. My friends are there. For now, I still have a house until my mother decides whether to sell it or rent it out."

She paused, then added reluctantly, "Jack and Betty Castro haven't exactly made it a secret that they would like me to go down to San Diego for a while so they and…their sons can get to know me beyond phone calls and emails."

He studied her out of those surprisingly perceptive brown eyes. "You're not so sure about that one, are you?"

She sighed, moving her undeniably delicious pasta around on her plate. At the reminder of the Castros, the happy bubble around them she suspected he had care-fully nurtured seemed to fizzle and pop.

"It's all so difficult. They're strangers to me, you know?"

"Sure they are." He paused and reached across the

table to entwine his fingers around hers. "You know, they're going to stay strangers to you until you make an effort to get to know them better."

"You sound like my mo—like Helen."

"Your mother," he said, squeezing her fingers lightly. "Helen is your mother, no matter what the DNA says."

His words brought a lump to her throat and she had to reach for her water glass. "My mother is urging me to spend more time with them."

"Don't you like them?"

"Sure I like them. They're very nice people."

How could she explain that spending time with them, coming to know them, would make this strange, twisted journey seem more real, somehow? She didn't understand her tangle of emotions, she only knew she wanted everything to go back to the way it was a few weeks ago, before she'd ever even heard of Erin Castro.

She couldn't continue in this limbo, she knew. Something had to change. She just wasn't sure she was ready yet.

"Jack and Betty are coming back to Thunder Canyon as soon as school lets out in San Diego to spend the holidays in Montana with Erin. Betty is a teacher there. History. Jack's a police officer. They have two sons in addition to Erin, one who's a police officer like his father and one who is a student."

"Are the brothers coming, too?"

"As far as I know, only Jack and Betty. They want to get to know me better while they're here."

"That's a start."

"We'll see."

She didn't want to talk about the Castros. She wanted that bright, happy bubble back. "What about you? What are your plans? Do you think you'll ever consider going back to law school?"

"Right now, I doubt it. I like working with my dad. I've discovered I really love the whole building process, seeing a place take shape under my direction. I'm not sure I'd get that same high from practicing law.

"So you think you'll be sticking around Thunder Canyon, then?"

He gave her another one of those intense, unreadable looks that made her blush, for reasons she didn't fully understand. "I guess you could say I'm pretty content with my life right now. For the most part, anyway."

She wondered if he was serious about the woman she'd seen him with the other night at dinner. Probably not. Matt probably had a dozen beautiful women like that, all eager to hang on his every word.

That probably shouldn't depress her so much, she thought. She wasn't doing a very effective job of protecting herself around him.

They finished eating a short time later and somewhat to Elise's surprise, she found she was grateful he'd parked some distance away so she could stretch out the enjoyable evening. He took her hand to help her over a patch of ice, then didn't release her. They walked hand in hand through the quiet streets.

She was fiercely aware of his heat seeping through her gloves, of his solid strength beside her.

She sighed, knowing perfectly well she shouldn't find such comfort just from his presence. Matt made her feel…safe. He had a tendency to watch out for anything smaller than he was but for some reason he had singled her out for extra protection.

She didn't know why but it seemed as if every time she found herself in trouble, Matt was there to help her out. Whether she was falling off a swing at the playground, tripping in the halls, schoolyard bullies, even suffering that flat tire last summer. Whenever she needed him, he seemed to be there.

What a comfort that was, she realized. A girl could definitely find herself getting used to that.

She had missed him after she moved away. Oh, she had made several good friends at her new high school in Billings, friends she kept to this day, but none who would step up to look out for her like Matt.

This time, they walked back to his truck by a more residential route, passing the small, close-set houses of downtown Bozeman. All seemed to be adorned with holiday decorations, from elaborately lit facades to a simple Christmas tree in the window and a wreath on the door. They were still a block from his pickup when Elise suddenly grabbed Matt's arm, peering around him to the shadows near a white clapboard house.

"What was that?"

He looked around. "What's the matter?"

"I saw something out of the corner of my eye. Something huge." She squinted in the direction of the blur, vaguely aware even as she did that Matt had moved his body protectively in front of her, even though he didn't know what she was talking about or even if anything posed a threat.

Maybe it was just a shadow. No. There it was again.

Her gaze sharpened and she gasped. "Do you see it?" she asked him. "Over there by the corner of that house across the street. Near that big pine tree."

He scanned the area and then laughed. "A moose! Right in the middle of town. Think he's Christmas shopping?"

"How cool is that?" she exclaimed. "I've seen plenty of mule deer in town, even in Billings, but never a moose."

She stood with her hand in Matt's, heedless of the cold seeping into her bones as they watched the massive creature leisurely nibble on a bush as if he were standing at the buffet at a Christmas party.

They watched for a long time, until Matt suddenly snickered. "He'd better watch out for the colored lights on the next bush or he's going to find himself a not-very-merry crisp moose."

She groaned and laughed at the same time. "Oh. You had to go and ruin a lovely moment with a lame joke."

"Sorry." He smiled at her and reached to push a loose strand of hair away from her face, his suede gloves caressing her skin.

"You need to do that more often," he murmured.

"What? Complain about your corny jokes? Sure. Anytime."

"I meant laugh. I've always thought you had the sweetest laugh of anyone I know."

She stared at him for a long moment, her heart pulsing. What would he do if she kissed him? Just reached up on tiptoe and pulled his head down to hers? The moment stretched out between them, as bright and hopeful as those fairy lights dripping from the eaves of the nearby house. She drew up on her toes inside her boots…then chickened out and slid back down to the ground.

"The people inside have no idea he's even out here," she said, her voice hushed.

He was quiet for a moment, then he spoke in an equally hushed voice. "It's amazing what you can miss when you're not paying attention."

Her gaze flashed again to his and her stomach trembled at the intensity in his eyes and a moment later, his mouth brushed hers.

His lips were warm and firm and he tasted of chocolate and mint from the piece of gourmet candy their server had delivered with their check at the restaurant.

She closed her eyes and leaned into his strength. The night seemed magical. The lights, the moose, the easy flutters of snow. She felt so safe here, warm and content, a slow peace soaking through her.

She finally followed her impulse of earlier and rose up on her toes so she could wrap her arms around his neck, savoring the heat of him.

She was in deep trouble. Since Friday night she had wondered what it would be like to kiss him again. To really kiss him this time, not when she was slightly tipsy from too many margaritas but when she was completely clearheaded and rational.

Now she knew exactly how his mouth tasted and his arms felt around her, exactly how silky his hair was sliding through her fingertips and the strength of his muscles against her body.

What she didn't know was how, in heaven's name, she would manage to endure the rest of her life without more of this—without more of *him*.

She shivered suddenly, cold despite his heat engulfing her, and Matt immediately slid his mouth away.

"You're freezing," he murmured. "I'm a brute to keep you out here in the cold."

She couldn't tell him her reaction wasn't from the temperature but from reality slapping her around. Better to let him think she was in danger of freezing to death than to admit she was afraid of having her heart broken.

"That's probably a good idea."

They left the moose to his browsing and Matt grabbed her hand to lead her the rest of the way to his truck.

A single kiss shouldn't leave him feeling as if his world had been rocked off its whole foundation.

A half hour later as Matt drove back to Thunder Canyon, his heartbeat still hadn't managed to settle. Every time he looked at Elise in the seat beside him, blond and delicate and lovely, he felt that little tingle of awareness, the urgent throb of hunger.

He felt as if everything in his world had changed. A week ago, he thought he had everything figured out. He was happy with his life in Thunder Canyon, content working for his dad.

And then Elise Clifton blew back into town and

everything he thought was important seemed to have shifted.

For a few moments after they had returned to his pickup, they had made small talk. But even before they left the Bozeman town limits, she started to yawn. Now she appeared to be fast asleep.

He risked another quick glance across the cab of the truck. She seemed comfortable enough with her cheek pressed against the upholstery but he still had to fight the urge to ease her onto his shoulder and tuck her under his arm, which wasn't the most safe position when the roads were slick and icy from the light snow.

He sighed. What was he supposed to do with her now?

He hadn't missed that when she was talking about her options for the future, not once had she mentioned staying and settling down in Thunder Canyon for good. She had talked about returning to Billings and about spending time with her newly discovered birth parents, but never anything about staying in town.

What would he have to do or say to convince her to add that to her plate of possibilities? he wondered.

He had a feeling he would have to take things slow and steady with her. Anticipation curled through him. He didn't mind. He could be patient when the payoff promised to be everything he had never realized he wanted.

He was still mulling his options when he finally drove up to the Clifton's Pride ranch house.

"Elise? Sweetheart, we're back."

Her eyes blinked open. For a few seconds, she stared

at him with a disoriented look in her eyes and then she gave him a slow smile that made him wish he was seeing it from the comfort of his own bed, with her on the pillow next to him, instead of in the cramped cab of his pickup truck.

"Hey," she murmured. "Sorry I fell asleep. It was a crazy day at ROOTS today. I never realized just how exhausting a bunch of teenagers could be. I guess I was more tired than I thought."

"No problem. It was warm and cozy in here. I don't blame you a bit. I would have liked to sleep, too."

"I'm really glad one of us decided to stay awake."

She reached to open her door, but he quickly held out a hand to stop her. "Thank you again for your help picking out Haley's gift. I don't know what I would have done without you. I think she's going to be very happy with it."

She smiled. "You're welcome. I... It was really a lovely evening."

He couldn't help himself. Despite all his plans to give her time, he had to kiss her again, especially when she looked so soft and sleepy and adorable.

He leaned across the width of the pickup and cupped her chin, then lowered his mouth to hers. She seemed to sigh against him, just about the sexiest sound he'd ever heard and after a long moment, he felt her arms around his neck.

The kiss was slow and gentle, like an easy ride into the mountains on a summer evening. He intended to keep it that way, but then her mouth parted slightly and he couldn't resist deepening the kiss.

She froze for just a moment and then she was kissing him back, her mouth eagerly dancing with his, her curves pressed against him.

After several long, delicious moments, she finally jerked away, her breathing ragged. Her knit cap had fallen off and her hair was tousled. She shoved it away from her face with fingers that trembled slightly.

Her mouth was swollen from his kiss and he drew his fingers into fists to keep from reaching for her again.

She stared at him for a long moment, then she shook her head, that curtain of hair swinging with the movement. "This really isn't a good idea."

He pretended to misunderstand, even as he felt a hard knot of unease lodge under his breastbone. "I know. Been a long time since I made out in the cab of a pickup truck. Seems a lot harder than it used to be."

"You know that's not what I meant."

"Elise—"

She shook her head. "Don't. Let me finish. I'm obviously attracted to you. I have been for, well, a long time. But I…I'm not in a very good place right now for a casual fling. I need to tell you that."

He opened his mouth to argue that he wanted much more than that but she again cut him off.

"I'm still trying to sort out everything that's happened the last few weeks and I'm afraid I really can't afford this sort of…of distraction right now."

"I can wait."

She looked stunned by his words but quickly shook her head. "I'm not asking you to wait. That's not fair to either of us. Matt, you've always been a great friend to me. I don't want to risk losing that by complicating everything."

Now there was a tidy little bit of irony. He eased back into his seat. How many times had he used similar phrases while trying to let a woman down gently? He didn't know quite how to react. Mostly he was confused. How could she kiss him with such sweet passion and then try to brush him off in the next moment?

"I think you're just trying to come up with any excuse to run away," he finally said.

She narrowed her gaze. "Oh?"

"I think you sense we could have something really fantastic together and that scares you right now so you're taking the safe road."

She looked out the window. "We might have been friends in grade school, Matt, but it's been years. I'm not the same person I was then. Don't make the mistake of thinking you know anything about me or about what I feel right now."

"I know enough to recognize when someone's running away. Believe me, I've been doing it long enough myself that I recognize all the signs. You're scared."

"And you're unbelievable." She reached for her door.

"Elise, don't. I'm sorry." He was blowing this. Hadn't he just vowed to give her whatever time and space she needed? Now here he was jumping on her for being cautious. He needed to back off. He could be patient, especially with something this important.

"Forget I said anything. You're right. The timing is

FREE Merchandise is 'in the Cards' for you!

Dear Reader,

We're giving away FREE MERCHANDISE!

Seriously, we'd like to reward you for reading this novel by giving you **FREE MERCHANDISE** worth over **$20**. And no purchase is necessary!

You see the Jack of Hearts sticker above? Paste that sticker in the box on the Free Merchandise Voucher inside. Return the Voucher promptly...and we'll send you valuable Free Merchandise!

Thanks again for reading one of our novels—and enjoy your Free Merchandise with our compliments!

Pam Powers

Pam Powers

P.S. Look inside to see what Free Merchandise is **"in the cards"** for you!

(S-SE-12/10)

W
e'd like to send you two free books to introduce you to the Silhouette Special Edition® series. These books are worth over $10, but they are yours to keep absolutely FREE! We'll even send you 2 wonderful surprise gifts. You can't lose!

REMEMBER: Your Free Merchandise, consisting of **2 Free Books** and **2 Free Gifts**, is worth over $20.00! No purchase is necessary, so please send for your Free Merchandise today.

YOUR FREE MERCHANDISE INCLUDES...

2 FREE Silhouette Special Edition® Books

AND 2 FREE Mystery Gifts

FREE MERCHANDISE VOUCHER

2 FREE BOOKS and **2 FREE GIFTS**

Please send my Free Merchandise, consisting of
2 Free Books and **2 Free Mystery Gifts**.
I understand that I am under no obligation to buy
anything, as explained on the back of this card.

*About how many NEW paperback fiction books
have you purchased in the past 3 months?*

☐ 0-2
E9EY

☐ 3-6
E9FC

☐ 7 or more
E9FN

235/335 SDL

Please Print

| |
| |

FIRST NAME

| |
| |

LAST NAME

| |
| |

ADDRESS

| | |
| | |

APT.#   CITY

| | |
| | |

STATE/PROV.   ZIP/POSTAL CODE

NO PURCHASE NECESSARY!

▲ If offer card is missing write to: The Reader Service, P.O. Box 1867, Buffalo, NY 14240-1867 or visit www.ReaderService.com ▲

BUSINESS REPLY MAIL
FIRST-CLASS MAIL   PERMIT NO. 717   BUFFALO, NY

POSTAGE WILL BE PAID BY ADDRESSEE

THE READER SERVICE
PO BOX 1867
BUFFALO NY 14240-9952

NO POSTAGE
NECESSARY
IF MAILED
IN THE
UNITED STATES

lousy. You want to be friends, we'll be friends. I'm fine with that. Come on, I'll walk you to the door."

"That's really not necessary."

He gave her a pointed look that seemed to shut her up in a hurry. They trudged through the thin skiff of snow to the porch of the ranch house. It was past midnight and most of the windows were dark, though someone had thoughtfully left a light burning on the porch for her and a colorful Christmas tree blazed from the front window.

"Please don't be mad at me, Matt," she said in a low voice when they approached the front door. "I really did have a great time with you tonight. More fun than I've had in…a while now."

"I'm not mad," he protested, though it wasn't quite true. He was mad at circumstances—at Erin Castro for stirring up the past, at her family for not seeing how upset and lost Elise was, at himself for the lunacy at falling for her right now when she had other things to cope with.

He would deal, he told himself. What other choice did he have?

"Good night." He forced himself to give her only a kiss on the cheek, even though he wanted much, much more, then he turned around and walked back through the cold.

While she removed her coat and scarf and slid off her boots, Elise kept her gaze fixed out the window, watching Matt turn his truck around in the driveway then head back in the direction of Thunder Canyon.

She watched until his taillights faded pink in the lightly falling snow and then disappeared.

She wanted suddenly to be the sort of woman he was probably used to, someone who could flirt and laugh and kiss without thinking anything of it. But kisses meant something to her. Especially *his* kisses. She couldn't pretend otherwise.

A month or two ago, she might have been happy just for the chance to indulge her foolish daydreams about him, even at the risk of a little inevitable heartbreak. He was Matt Cates, for heaven's sake.

But she didn't have room in her life for that sort of mess and chaos right now.

She made the right choice, she told herself as she walked into the kitchen for a glass of water before heading to her room. Friendship with him was a much more safe option than these tantalizing kisses and terrifying emotions.

She saw a light glowing from the kitchen and just assumed her mother or Stephanie had left it on for her. She walked in to turn it off and discovered her sister-in-law sitting at the kitchen table with a mug bearing a silly blue snowman in front of her.

"Hey, you!" Elise exclaimed softly. "What are you still doing up?"

Stephanie gave her a quick smile and Elise thought how happy she was that her brother and one of her dearest friends had found love together. They had been married for three years now and seemed happier than ever.

"I couldn't sleep," Steph said.

"Everything okay?"

Stephanie made a face. "The baby's restless tonight. He's rolling around like he's calf roping in there."

Elise forced a laugh. "Maybe the kiddo is practicing the pre-Christmas hijinks to get the parents psyched and ready for all the sleepless nights a few years from now when he's a little kid waiting for Santa."

"Oh, don't remind me of that." Steph gestured to her mug. "I'm already having nightmares about putting together toys on Christmas Eve. I had a craving for cinnamon hot cocoa and thought it might help me and the baby relax a little. Want to join me?"

"Think I'll pass on the cocoa but I'll keep you company for a minute."

She sank into a chair across from Stephanie, thinking again how very much she had always loved the kitchen at Clifton's Pride. After she and her mother moved to Billings, Elise had missed many things about the ranch. Moonlit rides into the mountains, the excitement of roundup, the thrill of watching a newborn foal come into the world.

One of the things she had missed most of all was this kitchen, warm and comfortable and homey.

Steph and Helen had decorated the kitchen for Christmas, with greenery and lights and pinecones covering every unused space. As she sat with her sister-in-law in the hush of a December evening, she could fully understand why Steph and Grant loved it here so much.

She reached down and rubbed her feet, sore from her long day at ROOTS and then their snowy walk through Bozeman. Better not to think about that, she told herself, especially if she wanted to stick to her resolve to be only friends with Matt.

"How was your evening?" her sister-in-law asked.

Her mind flashed to the two kisses she and Matt had shared, both very different but equally intense.

"Nice," she paused, then added in what she hoped was a casual tone, "I went to Bozeman with Matt Cates."

"Helen mentioned you left her a message on her cell phone that you were going with him."

Elise heard the curiosity in her friend's voice and she purposely avoided her eyes. Steph and Haley both knew she'd had a major crush on Matt when they were girls. They had all giggled about him and Marlon and the other cute boys often enough at recess and sleepovers.

"Matt was trying to pick out a Christmas present for Haley and he asked for my input," she said.

"Did you find something?"

"Yes. I took him to that gallery near Grand Avenue, the one with all the embroidery. We found a gorgeous piece with an eagle alighting with outstretched wings in an oak tree. It will go beautifully in the ROOTS clubhouse."

Stephanie's eyes lit up. "That does sound perfect. Haley will be thrilled."

"I think so. It fits perfectly with her concept for ROOTS, a place where teens can stretch their wings while remaining rooted to values and traditions."

"I didn't realize art galleries stayed open this late," Stephanie said.

Elise shot her a quick look but her sister-in-law merely sipped at her hot cocoa with an innocent look. "We went to dinner afterward at that steak house you and Grant took me to a few years ago."

Stephanie was quiet for a moment, then she looked at her with concern in her eyes. "I guess Matt's fiancée must be an understanding sort."

Elise froze as her heart gave one hard, brutal kick in her chest. "Sorry. His…what?"

Stephanie looked apologetic. "Well, I'm not sure it's official yet, but someone in town asked me about it today."

"I'm sure it was a mistake." Oh, heavens. Let it be a mistake. Fate wouldn't play that particularly nasty trick on her twice.

"I don't know. My source sounded pretty credible. Remember we saw him at dinner last night with Christine Mayhew? Tall, leggy brunette?"

"Yes," Elise said, her voice low. She remembered the woman vividly and the way she and Matt had appeared so cozy together.

"The mother of one of my riding students works at the front desk of Thunder Canyon Resort. Joanie Martin. After the lesson today, we were chatting about the party next week at the McFarlane Lodge and about how hard Matt and his father had rushed to finish it. In the course of the conversation, she asked me if I'd heard about Christine and Matt yet. She said she overheard Matt telling someone after dinner last night that he and Christine were making plans for their future together. Speculation is they're going to announce it at Connor's big party on Christmas Eve."

The dinner she had barely touched at the Bozeman

restaurant seemed to congeal into a hard, nasty ball inside her stomach. She thought of his kisses and the tenderness in his arms.

We could have something really fantastic together.

Had that just been a line? She tried to remember their conversation and realized he had never once said anything that implied he wanted anything more from her than the fling she'd accused him of wanting except for that—which in the abstract was vague enough it could mean anything. He could have just been talking about great sex, since they seemed to strike such sparks off each other.

Engaged. How could he be engaged? She wanted to deny it, to chide Stephanie for listening to gossip. But Steph wouldn't lie and she wouldn't repeat something unless she considered the source credible. Elise had seen them too, talking and laughing, had seen Matt's arm around the other woman.

Hadn't she always known he was a player? Oh, he might kiss her with breathtaking intensity but it obviously meant little to him.

She felt nauseous, remembering another time, another place, when she had been forced to stand politely by while the man she thought she loved, the one she had given her virginity to just a few weeks earlier, had introduced her to his very lovely bride to be.

Was it really possible that she had completely misread the situation with Matt? Now she couldn't meet Stephanie's concerned gaze, afraid of what her sister-in-law might read in her foolish, foolish eyes.

"Matt and I are just friends," she mumbled, wondering why her lips suddenly felt numb and achy.

Friends. The word rang hollow. She certainly couldn't consider any man a friend who would put her in this position—and worse, when he would betray his fiancée with such callous disregard.

How foolish she was, still hanging on to childish dreams. That she would even consider for a moment that Matt might genuinely have feelings for her made her just about the most pitiful woman in the county.

For just a moment, she fought down a vicious stab of jealousy that some other woman would know the sweetness of those kisses, the strength of his arms, the tenderness of his lying, cheating smile.

"I'm sorry, El," Steph said.

She forced her own smile, hoping it looked more genuine than it felt.

"About what? Matt and I are friends," she repeated. Friends who neglect to mention an impending engagement. Who laugh and tease and kiss and betray.

"Whether he's engaged or not is no business of mine," she lied. "He needed a favor, I owed him one for rescuing me the other night at The Hitching Post. Now we're square. He's free to be engaged to a dozen women, as far as I'm concerned."

Steph didn't quite look convinced. Small wonder, since Elise couldn't even convince herself.

"You know, I'm beat. Think I'll leave you to your cocoa and the quiet. I wouldn't want to get the little one riled up again now that you've calmed him down."

Stephanie smiled a little but touched Elise's hand with concern still in her eyes.

"It's really been wonderful having you back here at the ranch. Just like old times. I don't think I've told you that enough since you came back."

Tears pricked the back of her eyelids as she hugged her sister-in-law and friend. She told herself it was just exhaustion from the busy day. "It's fun to watch you growing that baby in there. You're going to be a great mom, Steph."

Stephanie made a face. "We'll see about that. I have a lot to learn. But at least I can make a mean cup of hot cocoa."

Elise forced a smile and said good-night, then headed for her bedroom—the same one she had used when she was a girl, before her father's murder, when life at Clifton's Pride was warm and joyful.

By the time she closed the door behind her and sagged onto her bed with its blue-and-violet quilt, she was shaking with anger and something else, something dark and forlorn.

The anger was wholly justified. But she had no business entertaining even for a moment this yawning sense of betrayal, of loss.

Matt had never been hers. Not a half hour ago, she had bluntly told him she wasn't interested in a relationship. How pathetic must that had sounded to him, when he obviously wasn't interested in anything so formal, anyway?

She had a lucky escape, she reminded herself. Some wise part of her had warned her not to let herself be swept away by the moment, by the seductive magic of being in his arms.

Good thing she had listened to it and hadn't done something supremely foolish like allow her heart to get tangled up with his.

Right?

Chapter Eight

"You're sure everything will be ready by the end of the week so we can bring in the decorators?" Connor McFarlane surveyed the kitchen where Matt was currently installing the knobs and handles on the custom cabinetry.

"That's the plan," Matt answered, carefully setting another hole. "Everything is on schedule. The carpet layers will be here tomorrow and we'll do the floor trim and hang the closet systems the day after that, and that should wrap it all up."

"Good. Excellent. I've got a team of designers coming in from McFarlane House hotels to finish up and they've informed me they need at least four days."

"We should be good," Matt said again. Better than

good. He loved a job well done. Finishing that job ahead of schedule was icing on the cake.

Connor ran a hand over the Italian marble countertops. "Cates Construction has gone above and beyond to bring the work in early. I want you to know I won't forget the work you've done here."

"It's been a pleasure." The words might seem polite but Matt sincerely meant them and he hoped Connor knew it.

He was proud to have his name associated with this particular construction project. McFarlane Lodge would be a showpiece in Thunder Canyon, tasteful and well-crafted. More than that, it would be warm and comfortable, a home for Connor, his son CJ and his wife to be, Tori Jones.

The only thing he loved more than setting the last tile and hammering the final nail was the other side of any building project: that first scoop of dirt in the backhoe, those heady days of pouring the foundation and framing the first few walls, when everything was still only possibilities.

He was particularly pleased about the chance to be part of building McFarlane Lodge, with its expansive views and the massive river-rock fireplace that served as the focal point in the open floor plan.

"I've got other irons in the fire around Thunder Canyon," Connor said with a significant look. "I'm going to need a dependable contractor. I'd love to keep Cates Construction at the top of that list."

Matt experienced a sharp burst of pride and a not inconsiderable degree of elation. He didn't doubt that the hotel magnate had various projects underway. Connor always seemed to be cooking up something and in this economy, anything that allowed Cates Construction to keep its workers swinging a hammer was a blessing.

"If we can fit in the job with our other commitments, we'll be happy to consider whatever work you send our way," he said, moving on to the next cabinet.

Connor smiled and patted the countertop. "I'm sure we can work something out. I'll be in touch."

"Sure thing."

After McFarlane left the kitchen a moment later, Matt glanced toward the adjacent laundry room. A grizzled gray buzz cut bobbed there and he could see his father lurking, pretending not to listen.

"You catch all that, Dad?" he asked with a grin.

Frank walked into the kitchen. "I heard. He's right. You've done a hell of a job with the place."

"This isn't a one-man show. The whole crew worked their tails off to get 'er done by Christmas."

"Don't be humble, son." Frank gave him a stern look. "It doesn't fit you. You're the one who made it happen on time and under budget and every single man on the crew knows it."

Matt flushed at the unexpected accolades. Frank was a good man and a wonderful father but he wasn't one for outright praise—his style was more like subtle encouragement. Matt didn't know quite how to respond.

"You've done so well the last few years, you're starting to put ideas in your mother's head."

Matt looked up and found his father looking remarkably ill at ease. "Oh? What sort of ideas?"

"Crazy ones." Frank sighed. "She's talking about taking a cruise. Maybe even a couple of them. She's even brought up maybe heading somewhere warm for the winter. Southern Utah, maybe, or Arizona. You know how the cold bothers her."

The idea of a Thunder Canyon without his parents was just too strange to contemplate. "What do you think about her ideas?"

His father was silent for a long moment. "I'm considering them. I've been in this business a long time. I've got old habits, old ways. Maybe it's time somebody else shook some new life into Cates Construction."

"Dad—"

"Your brothers aren't much interested in construction, son. Marshall's busy at the hospital and Mitch and Marlon both have their own companies. I don't suppose it's a surprise to you or any of them that I would like you to take over for me. Hell, you're doing most of the work, anyway. I'd just like to make it more official."

Excitement pulsed through him. This was what he wanted, he realized. Taking over the operations of Cates Construction fit him much better than law school ever could.

"I would have asked you before but I didn't want you to feel tied down to Thunder Canyon. You're still young. Your mother and I have always wanted you boys to feel free to experience the world on your own terms, not ours. But now that it looks like you're settling down, I figured this would be a good time to get things out in the open."

Matt stared. "Now that I'm what?"

His father looked uncomfortable. "Your mother's got some crazy idea you're getting married."

"Where did you hear that?" he asked.

"Apparently Edie heard a rumor last night at her bunco club about you," he answered. "A couple different people dropped a bug in her ear that you and Christine are talking about tying the knot."

The hammer suddenly slipped out of his fingers and he barely managed to snag it before it would have clattered onto the Italian tile floor.

He mentally hissed an expletive he wouldn't dare say aloud in front of his father. He should have known his impulsive gesture Sunday at The Gallatin Room would come back to bite him in the rear one day. He hadn't been thinking clearly or he never would have started the charade.

What the hell was he supposed to say to his father now?

"Um, don't believe everything you hear, Dad. Christine and I aren't getting married."

Frank narrowed his gaze. "What are you up to, son?"

"Nothing. This is all a big misunderstanding."

"I thought I taught you boys better than to mess around when it comes to this sort of thing."

"You did. I haven't been messing around."

Frank cleared his throat, looking ill at ease. "A woman's heart is a fragile thing, son. It's like that tile down there. If you'd dropped your hammer a minute ago, you might have chipped one of them fancy tiles. We might have repaired it, filled it in a bit. On the surface, it might look good as new, but there would always be a weakness there."

His father gave him a stern look. "Christine is a nice girl. If you're not serious about her, you need to cut her loose so she can find somebody who will be."

He did *not* want to be having this conversation with his father right now. "I hear you, Dad. Thanks for the advice."

"So you're going to do the right thing by Christine?"

"If by doing the right thing you mean marry her, then no. Trust me, Dad. Christine is not expecting an engagement ring from me. We're good friends, that's all."

His father continued to study him. "I hope you're right. I guess I need to tell your mother she won't be planning another wedding anytime soon."

For one insane moment, Matt pictured Elise in a white dress, something feminine and lovely, flowers in her blond hair and her face bright and joyful.

Whoa. Slow down. He drew in a sharp breath, astonished at the yearning trickling through him.

He wasn't at all ready to go there yet. Even if *he* was—which he clearly wasn't, right?—Elise certainly had made it apparent the night before that she didn't want to have anything with him beyond friendship.

That seductive image faded like an old photograph under a hard western sun. He had his work cut out for him to convince her he wanted more. But Matt had never been the sort to back down from a challenge.

* * *

Three hours later, Matt drove through town on his way to drop off a bid at a restaurant in Old Town Thunder Canyon that was planning a big remodeling project.

If the restaurant just happened to be on the same street as ROOTS, well, that was a happy coincidence. It would give him a chance to implement his new strategy for winning Elise over.

She claimed she didn't want to lose their friendship. Great. Fine. He had decided he would be the best damn friend she'd ever had. He would offer a sympathetic ear, a helping hand, a shoulder—whatever part of his anatomy she needed, until she discovered she didn't know how she could survive without him.

Though it was a weekday afternoon, Christmas shoppers were out in force in town. He happened to spy Bo Clifton and his very pregnant wife Holly heading into a clothing store, and Tori Jones and Allaire Traub coming out of the florists with their arms full of what looked like poinsettias and evergreen branches.

After he dropped off the bid to the restaurant owner, he dodged holiday shoppers and slushy snow piles down the street a few storefronts to the ROOTS clubhouse.

Connor McFarlane's son CJ sat with Ryan Chilton and a couple of other boys at one of the tables with textbooks open in front of them, though they didn't seem to be paying them much attention. A couple of teen girls he didn't know looked bored as they leafed through magazines on the couch.

As he had hoped, Elise was at Haley's desk, the

phone pressed to her ear. Her gaze lifted at the sound of the bells on the door chiming, a ready smile on her features.

The moment she spied him coming through the door, her smile slid away and her expression turned stony, much to his consternation.

He eased into the chair across from the desk. By the time she finished her phone call, her eyes were the wintry blue of the Montana sky on a clear January afternoon and her jaw looked set in concrete.

She hung up the phone, a muscle twitching in her cheek. "Can I help you?"

Not a good sign, when her voice was even colder than her eyes.

"Um, I was in the neighborhood dropping off a bid and figured I'd walk down and see if you need help filling the gift bags."

"They're done," she said curtly. "I finished them today."

This wasn't going at all as he'd hoped. "Okay, then. Any idea what my assignment might be for the Christmas party? Haley said something about needing some muscle for setting up tables, that sort of thing."

"I don't know. You'll have to ask her that."

"I'm assuming since you're here and she's not that she's still laid low with the flu," he hazarded a guess.

Elise jerked her head in a nod. "She sounded better this morning when she called. She should be back tomorrow. I'm sure you can talk to her then."

So much for his grand master plan. Elise was acting as if she didn't even want to share the same air space with him. The night before, she had said she didn't want to lose their friendship. Had he screwed that up now?

"What's wrong?" he finally asked warily. "You seem upset."

She made the same sort of sound his mother did when he tracked job-site mud on her mopped floors. "Do I?"

He looked around the ROOTS clubhouse to make sure none of the teens were paying attention to them, then he leaned forward. "Is this about last night?"

Her jaw hardened even more and for a long moment, he didn't think she would answer him. When she spoke, the chill in her voice was nearing arctic proportions.

"I suppose you could say that. You put me in a terrible position."

He glanced at the teens, who seemed to be arguing about some super-hero movie and paying absolutely no attention to them.

"Why? Because I kissed you?" he asked in a low voice. "You weren't complaining at the time."

Whoops. Wrong thing to say. The ice queen disappeared in an instant. Elise shoved her chair back and rose, her color high. He wouldn't have expected it, but apparently his quiet, sweet Elise could pack a pretty decent temper.

"You haven't changed a bit," she snapped. "You're the same wild, irresponsible cowboy who thinks he can use his charm to get away with anything!"

Where did that come from? "Hold it right there," he said, pitching his voice low. "What the hell did I do?"

"You kissed me!" she hissed.

That drew the attention of the teens. A couple of them—the girls especially—cast sidelong looks in their direction. Maybe this conversation would be better in private, he thought, about five minutes too late.

He gestured with his head to the teens and then pointed to a back room. Mortification replaced some of the anger in her eyes but she gave a short nod and headed into the back room, closing the door behind them.

"I guess I haven't read the Thunder Canyon town or-dinances closely enough," Matt said when they had some measure of privacy. "I didn't realize kissing a beautiful woman had been outlawed when I wasn't looking."

Two high spots of color flared on her cheeks. "It might not be a crime, but it's wrong on so many levels I don't even know where to start."

"Why?"

"You're engaged to marry someone else!"

He stared at her for about twenty seconds. He closed his eyes, cursing his big mouth and the white knight syndrome he couldn't seem to shake.

"This is about Christine?"

"Of *course* it's about Christine! I can't believe you even have to ask! I always knew you were a player, I just never imagined you would take things this far."

He had a feeling this was a disclaimer he was going to have to provide a few times before the rumors around Thunder Canyon started to fade. "I'm not engaged to Christine. I never was. We're only friends."

"Funny, that's not the rumor going around town. The minute I walked in the house last night, Stephanie was bending my ear about your engagement. And she's not the only one. I've now heard it from more than one person."

He loved living in Thunder Canyon but life in a small town where everybody cared about your business had some definite downfalls. A stray bit of gossip could run rampant like an August wildfire. With just a little fuel, it would spread to every corner, wreaking havoc in its path.

And he had stupidly been the one to set the match to this particular rumor. He should have expected this, damn it.

The hell of it was, he couldn't go around putting out this particular fire completely, not if Christine was going to convince her jackass of an ex that they were done.

He might not be able to tell everyone, but he could certainly confide the truth to Elise, he decided. "Look, if I tell you something, I need you to keep it to yourself, at least for a little while."

She crossed her arms over her chest, obviously not at all in the mood to listen to anything he had to say. Still, she didn't toss him out so he figured he would take what he could get at this point.

"The truth is, Christine had an overenthusiastic ex-boyfriend a few months back who couldn't seem to get the message they were really over. I wouldn't exactly put him in the stalker category, but maybe a step or two down from that. She confided in me one night what she'd been going through and somehow we decided to pretend to be dating in hopes the ex would finally figure out it was over."

"So out of the goodness of your heart, you agreed to pretend to date a beautiful woman with absolutely pure and altruistic motives."

He fought down annoyance at her sharp tone. "I never said that. I'll be honest, it was a mutually beneficial arrangement. My parents stopped bugging me for a while about settling down for the first time since Haley and Marlon got together. And I enjoy Christine's company. She's a very fun person. But we're not engaged and never will be. Neither of us feels that way about the other."

She didn't look convinced. "For the sake of argument, let's say I was stupid enough to believe you. Don't you think becoming engaged to the woman is taking your charade a little too far?"

He sighed. How to explain this part without sounding like a complete idiot? "We bumped into a cousin of the ex-boyfriend outside The Gallatin Room the other night. Completely on the spur of the moment, I figured this was the perfect opportunity to convince the guy things were over, once and for all. I never really stopped to consider the consequences, that word might trickle out and we would have to explain the truth someday."

He thought he detected a slight thaw in her expression but it was barely perceptible so he pressed harder.

"I'm telling the truth, Elise. Come on, think about it. Do you really believe I'm the kind of guy who would announce his engagement one night, then spend the next night kissing someone else?"

She gave him a long, considering look. "I can't answer that, Matt. I guess that's part of the problem. I've been away from Thunder Canyon for a long time. All

I know are the rumors I've heard about your wild past. Didn't you and Marlon get engaged a few years ago to twins you'd barely met?"

He winced. She *would* have to dredge up that little gem of a story, one of his less than stellar moments. "We were young and stupid. I think it was more of a joke than anything. Marlon and I have both changed over the years. Look at him, happily engaged to Haley. And he was always the reckless one, not me. I was mostly along for the ride."

He thought the ice thawed just a little more. At least she didn't look ready to feed him to the wolves yet.

"Trust your instincts, El," he said softly, reaching for her hand. "We're friends. I wouldn't treat any woman like that, not Christine and not you."

She stared at him for a long moment and he could feel the tremble of her slender fingers. She swallowed hard and opened her mouth to say something, but at that moment the door was shoved open.

CJ McFarlane burst in, all auburn hair and lanky skater boy. He didn't seem to notice any of the fine-edged tension in the room. "We're starving, Miz Clifton. Okay if we nuke a couple bags of popcorn? Haley keeps a supply back here."

"Um, sure." She stepped away from Matt and tucked a strand of hair behind her ear. "Anything else you need?"

"No. Popcorn ought to do it."

She gave Matt a long look, then returned to the other room. He followed, frustrated and more than a little annoyed that she was being so stubborn.

"I guess I'll give Haley a call about what she needs me to do for the party. Sorry I bothered you," he said tersely and headed for the door.

"Matt. Wait."

He turned. "Yeah?"

She twisted her fingers together and chewed her bottom lip. "What was I supposed to think?" she finally said with a quick look at the kids. "Stephanie's not the sort to make up stories."

"And I'm not the sort to string two women along. You ought to know me better than that."

She sighed. "I've been in that position before, in college. The other woman, I mean. My first real boyfriend was a…well, a jerk. I dated him for three months and never knew he had been engaged for a year to marry a girl in his hometown right after graduation. Then I bumped into them one day while they were picking out wedding flowers and had to stand there, stunned and heartbroken, while he introduced me as some girl he had a class with."

She paused, fidgeting with a stapler on Haley's desk. "It was an awful situation. I hated thinking you could do the same thing to me or to Christine."

He sighed. He felt like he was doing nothing but taking one step forward and two or three giant steps backward with her.

"I'm sorry you were hurt that way. But I'm not some idiot you knew in college, Elise. You've known me for a long time. You should have given me a chance to explain before you jumped to all kinds of crazy conclusions."

He was hurt, he realized. It was a feeling he wasn't

very accustomed to when it came to his dealings with women.

"I've got to go." He didn't want her to see it, didn't want to reveal the depth of his feelings for her just yet, not when she was fighting him every step of the way. "Tell Haley I dropped by and I'll do whatever she needs me to for the party."

"Matt—"

He didn't wait for whatever else she wanted to say, only pushed open the door and walked out of the ROOTS clubhouse and into the December afternoon that seemed to have lost all its good cheer.

Chapter Nine

"Everything looks absolutely perfect!"

Haley slung her arm over Elise's shoulders and pulled her close as they stood in the doorway admiring the winter wonderland they had spent all day creating in the ROOTS clubhouse.

"You did a fantastic job with the whole thing. You should be a party planner, El. You didn't need me after all," Haley said.

"Not true. I never could have thrown it all together without you the last two days. I still think you're overdoing it, though. Are you sure you're up to this?"

"I'm feeling almost back to normal, if I can only shed this stupid cough." As if to illustrate her point, she suddenly had to step away from Elise in order to cough into the corner of her sleeve.

"Sorry. I really am feeling better," she said after a moment. "Those garlands you made are fantastic and the swag bags are perfect."

"The kids are going to have a great time." She smiled at her friend, noting all the changes in Haley over the last few months. Her friend glowed with happiness, even though she still looked pale and worn-out from her illness.

Elise was thrilled for her. Haley's handbag design business, HA! was taking off, she was passionately committed to the success of ROOTS and she was deeply in love with Marlon Cates, who loved her right back.

She deserved all those wonderful things and more after giving up her dreams early in order to take care of her younger siblings after her single mother's untimely death.

Elise wouldn't have begrudged her any of it and she refused to feel even a tiny niggle of envy that everything seemed to be coming together so perfectly for Haley when Elise's life seemed like such a tangled mess.

"What you're doing here is a good thing, Haley. It's been really cool to be a part of it this week, in my small way."

"Not small." Haley squeezed her arm with affection. "You know we would have had to cancel the whole thing if you hadn't stepped in to save the day. I can't begin to tell you how much I appreciate it."

"I had help," Elise said. "Your hardworking volunteers plus those amazing kids."

"They are, aren't they? Amazing, I mean. I think I

get more out of associating with them than the other way around."

She looked at the clock suddenly. "And speaking of the kids, they're going to be here any minute now. You're staying, right? I won't let you leave, not after all your hard work."

Elise nodded. "I brought some party clothes to change into so I didn't have to go back to the ranch to change."

"See, that's why you always were the smartest girl I know."

Ha, Elise thought as she headed for the ROOTS women's restroom. If she were as smart as Haley thought, she would have stayed far away from Matt Cates the moment she spied him at The Hitching Post the other night. Instead, she had let her life become more and more entwined with his and now here she was fighting down completely inappropriate anticipation at the likely possibility that he would come to the party.

Not that he would be thrilled to see her. The last time she had seen him, the anger in his eyes that she had believed he was two-timing his fiancée by kissing Elise would have melted every inch of snow on the whole road out front.

She hadn't seen him in four days, since that tense scene here. His outrage still seemed unfair. If he was telling the truth—and she still hadn't managed to completely convince herself of that, despite every instinct that urged her to believe him—he and Christine Mayhew *wanted* people to think they were engaged, right?

Or at least one particular person, Christine's ex-boyfriend.

For him to be angry with Elise for believing the rumors they had started themselves seemed wrong, somehow.

She changed quickly, out of jeans and a hooded sweatshirt into a pair of black slacks and a shimmery white blouse, sheer at the neck and sleeves, then sighed as she replaced the utilitarian small hoops she'd put in her ears that morning with her favorite chunky, dangly crystals.

Why did it matter if Matt was upset with her? Engaged or not, her reasons for stopping their kiss the other night at Clifton's Pride remained. Nothing had changed since Monday. If anything, things were more tangled than ever now that Jack and Betty Castro were returning to Thunder Canyon for the holidays.

She thought of the phone call she had received the night before from Betty and her stomach quivered with nerves.

Betty and Jack were back in Montana, staying with friends in Billings. Betty had sounded desperately eager for Elise to join them for dinner on Sunday. She knew they genuinely wanted to get to know her, to forge whatever relationship they could with her.

Elise had always considered herself a nice person. She tried to treat people with decency and respect. But the Castros' continued overtures made her want to saddle up one of the Clifton's Pride horses and ride fast and hard into the mountains to hide out somewhere she wouldn't be found for days.

Her reaction was ridiculous, she knew, and rather shameful. The Castros weren't trying to hurt her. They only wanted to become acquainted with the child who had been taken from them by circumstances beyond anyone's control.

After she applied a new coat of mascara, Elise gazed in the mirror at the face she had seen looking back for twenty-six years. She had inherited her cheekbones, her eyes, the curve of her mouth from Betty and Jack. Didn't she owe it to them to at least be cordial?

She had two brothers she didn't know, an entire family history to learn. She couldn't keep avoiding them, hoping this whole tangled mess would just sort itself out. It was time to face her angst.

But not tonight. This was a Christmas party and she wouldn't ruin it for the teens that Haley helped.

The first guests had started to arrive by the time Elise finished changing her clothes and makeup. Haley had started playing some holiday music and Elise could see a group of teens already taking to the small dance floor they had set up.

She could see Haley's siblings, Austin and Angie, as well as many of the volunteers and teens she had become acquainted with the past week, including CJ McFarlane, Roy Robbins and Ryan Chilton.

Marlon was helping Haley fiddle with the speakers.

And Matt. Her insides did a long, slow roll when she spotted him filling glasses with punch at the refreshments table.

He looked dark and rugged and absolutely gorgeous in a dark green sweater, tan slacks and boots.

He wasn't alone, Haley suddenly realized. Next to him was the lovely brunette she recognized from the restaurant the other night, though that seemed a lifetime ago.

Christine Mayhew.

They were talking and laughing but she had to admit they looked more friendly than romantic. Was it possible he was telling the truth? She wanted to believe him. The last three days she hadn't heard any more rumors about any engagement—but she hadn't heard anything about it being a sham, either.

Haley suddenly grabbed her arm, distracting her from any more pointless wondering. "Help! I can't find the MP3 player I spent hours loading with a Christmas dance mix while I was sick," Haley wailed. "Have you seen it?"

"Is it your pink one? I think I saw it on the table in the back room. Let me go see if I can find it."

She supposed it wasn't a very good sign when she couldn't wait to leave a party not three minutes after she showed up. She hurried to the other room and emerged a moment later with the MP3 player in her hand.

Haley hugged her. "You're a lifesaver! We would have had to listen to 'Jingle Bell Rock' all night."

"Oh, horrors!"

Her friend laughed and headed back to Marlon and the sound system. Elise was just about to go talk to Austin and Angie when she saw Christine Mayhew heading in her direction.

The other woman was indeed beautiful, tall and curvy. Elise felt about twelve years old in contrast.

She wasn't at all prepared when Christine gave her a warm, friendly smile. "You're Elise Clifton, right?"

"Yes," she admitted warily.

"I'm Christine Mayhew. Matt's told me a lot about you."

"Has he?"

Christine's smile was warm and open and not the slightest bit jealous. "I have to tell you, I've never seen him like this about any other woman."

She stared. "Like...what?"

"Nothing. Sorry. Forget I said anything." Christine sent an amused look over her shoulder to where Matt was watching them intently. "I'm on a very important mission here tonight."

"Oh?"

"I'm under strict orders to convince you beyond a sliver of doubt that Matt and I are not engaged."

Elise cast a quick look at Matt then shifted her gaze away. She knew perfectly well she shouldn't have this little fizz of happiness welling up inside at the word.

"Matt is a great guy," Christine went on. "Don't get me wrong. I care about him and always will. But there won't be any wedding bells ringing for the two of us. We're friends, that's all. I swear it."

What was she supposed to say in response? *I'm really happy to hear that* didn't seem quite appropriate under the circumstances.

"He was doing me a favor," the other woman said firmly.

"Why are you telling me this?"

"Matt asked me to. He told me he explained it all to you but you still had some doubts."

"What about your ex-boyfriend?"

Christine shrugged. "Word on the street is that he's started dating someone else recently. I can only hope she turns out to be a keeper for him so he'll take my number off his speed dial."

She paused and studied Elise until she could feel her face heat in another of those blasted blushes. "Can I give you some advice?"

"Okay," she said slowly.

"I've been friends with Matt for a while now and as I said, I've never seen him like this over any woman." Christine gave her a careful smile. "I think you're more important to him than even he wants to admit."

Elise shot him another look. Though he was busy talking to his twin brother, he must have felt the weight of her stare because he shifted his attention to her. For a moment they stared at each other and the crowd, the decorations, the music all seemed to fade.

"Matt is a great guy. When he finally falls for a woman, I have a feeling he will move heaven and earth to make her feel happy and safe and loved."

Elise drew in a shaky breath. She didn't know what to say. She did know she shouldn't be fighting this powerful yearning to be that woman.

"Pretending to be his girlfriend these last few months has been great fun," Christine added, her glittery earrings reflecting the Christmas lights from the tree. "I can only imagine being the real thing would be a million times better."

With that parting shot, she walked away, leaving Elise floundering for a response.

For the next hour, she carefully avoided Matt as she circulated among the party guests and helped Haley with hostess duties. She knew she owed him an apology for ever doubting him but the middle of a noisy, festive party full of teenagers didn't quite seem the proper venue.

She was in the kitchen preparing another plate of appetizers when she finally couldn't avoid him any longer.

He walked in and something unreadable flashed in his gaze when he spotted her there. "I'm under orders from Haley to see if there are any more of those cheesy cream puff thingies in here."

"A few. I was just about to carry them out."

"Here, I can take them." She handed him the tray but instead of heading back out to the party, he stood in the doorway.

"It's a great party, Elise. Haley's giving you all the credit."

"Not true," she protested. "She had already laid all the groundwork. I only had to finalize a few details."

"Well, you did a great job. Everyone seems to be having a wonderful time, from the kids to their parents to the volunteers. And I know fundraising wasn't the intent of the party but Haley said donations have been pouring in."

She could barely focus on anything but Christine's words. *I've never seen him like this about another woman.*

She had to be wrong. He was treating her just like

he treated everyone else. Maybe even on the cold side of the politeness thermostat.

"More donations are always good."

He gave a short laugh and set the plate of appetizers back down on the counter. "Yeah, they are. Haley has done wonders with a small amount of money. Who knows what she can accomplish when her funds increase?"

He paused and gave her a careful look. "So do you want to tell me why you sound like I just told you somebody injected botulism into the cream puff thingies?"

She blinked, then flushed. "I'm happy about the donations. I just…I…I owe you an apology."

"I guess you've talked to Christine."

She sighed. "She was only corroborating what I already knew. I believed you that day you came here to ROOTS and explained about your sham engagement."

He winced. "It was never supposed to go that far, I swear it. I didn't expect anyone else to hear about it. I'm sorry you were caught up in it. The whole thing was stupid."

Christine was right, Elise realized. Matt was a good man. When he gave his heart, he would give it completely. He would never betray the woman he loved for some thrill *du jour*.

He couldn't be more different than her first boyfriend.

She drew in a deep breath, her pulse racing. "Christine basically told me I would be crazy if I didn't…give things with you a chance."

He gazed down at her but said nothing for several

long moments. The party sounds were muted in here, just a throb of bass, and she could swear she heard her heart beating in her ears, keeping time to the music.

"Are you going to listen to her?" he finally asked.

She swallowed hard and realized just where they were both standing—under one of the many clumps of mistletoe the kids had hung for the party.

"I'm thinking about it," she murmured, then without giving herself time to second-guess, she rose on tiptoes and brushed his mouth with hers.

He froze for just a moment, his mouth firm and delicious against hers, and then he made a low sound in his throat and kissed her back with a slow and aching gentleness.

Both of them kept their eyes open and she was hypnotized by the deep brown of his eyes as he stared back at her, unsmiling.

In that instant, she made a decision, what felt like a monumental one to her.

She eased away and gave him a tentative smile. "Would you like to go to Billings Sunday with me to have dinner with my...with Jack and Betty Castro?"

He looked as if he hadn't quite heard her right. "You want me to go with you while you have dinner with your birth parents?"

She nodded, feeling edgy and foolish and wondering if she was crazy to even ask. "To be honest, I think I could use a friend on my side there. But more than that, I really would like to...spend time with you. If you want to, anyway. I thought it would give us a little time to talk, on the way there and back."

She sounded like a complete idiot. Why couldn't she be smart and sophisticated, someone like Christine?

But Matt didn't seem to mind. His eyes were warm and he seemed to know exactly how difficult she had found it to ask him.

"That sounds terrific. Really terrific, as long as you're sure the Castros won't mind if I tag along."

"I don't think they will."

"Great. It's a date."

A date. She did a little mental gulp but it was too late to back down now.

"We'd better get these appetizers in there before those teenage boys start eating the popcorn strings I worked so hard on."

"Good idea."

He grabbed the plate and they headed back into the reception area.

Christine was sitting at a table talking to Erika Traub and a very pregnant Holly Clifton. She smiled when she saw them emerge from the kitchen together but Elise was painfully aware of a few speculative looks zinging between the two of them and Christine.

When news started to filter out of Matt's "breakup" with Christine, speculation was bound to fly that perhaps Elise was the cause of it. The thought of being the subject of more gossip filled her with dread and for a moment she was tempted to tell Matt to forget about everything.

No. She was tougher than that. She could withstand gossip. Hadn't she been doing it since her father's murder?

Matt smiled at her and she resolved to forget about everything for the rest of the night, to simply enjoy the party.

It was long past time she found a little holiday spirit.

Chapter Ten

"What was your favorite subject in school?"

Elise took a sip from her water glass at the elegant restaurant in Billings, doing her best to handle what felt very much like an interrogation. Beside her, Matt nudged his knee against hers and out of the corner of her gaze, she took great comfort from his supportive smile.

"Um, English," she finally answered. "I've always loved to read. Working in a bookstore is a dream come true."

That was apparently the perfect thing to say to a high school teacher. Betty's eyes warmed and her smile widened. "You come by that naturally, my dear. Women on my side of the family have always been big readers.

My mother, my aunts. All of us. They're all dying to meet you, by the way."

Oh, mercy. Elise hadn't given much thought to extended relatives she might have to meet. Aunts, uncles, cousins. Just the thought of it had her snatching up her water glass again and gulping it like she had just run a marathon through the Mojave.

Under the table, she felt Matt's leg nudge her knee again. He was doing it on purpose, she knew, offering her whatever physical comfort she could take from his touch.

"So Jack, tell me about being a police officer in San Diego. Harbor police, isn't it?" Matt asked as smoothly as the attorney he might have become, finessing a witness. "You probably deal with some really fascinating cases. What were you working on just before you came out to Montana?"

"My partner and I are trying to nail a money launderer working with the Mexican cartels. It's mostly legwork but we've had some close calls."

With Matt's subtle encouragement, all through their entrées Jack told stories about his work while Betty added her own perspective about what life was like being married to a police officer.

Elise liked both of them. They seemed to be a genuinely nice couple who loved each other and their family. That was one of the toughest things about everything that had happened. If circumstances had been different, she would very much have enjoyed the chance to get to know them.

Jack was just like the delicious cheese rolls they

served at the restaurant…crusty on the outside but warm and gooey at heart. Betty was smart and funny with a deep streak of kindness Elise had already sensed.

They seemed great, two people she instinctively wanted to know better. But everyone just seemed to expect so much of her.

Maybe it was only her. Erin didn't seem to be having the same trouble adjusting to everything. From the moment Erin met Helen and Grant, she seemed to instantly love them and had melded into the fiber of their family with apparent ease, with none of this stiff awkwardness Elise felt around her birth parents.

Elise knew she couldn't love them as parents and probably never would. Helen and John were her parents and no amount of DNA testing would ever change that, just as Matt kept trying to tell her. She just wished she could relax and become more comfortable with Jack and Betty's eagerness to be part of her life.

She just had to try harder, she told herself. "How long will you be staying in Montana?" she asked at the next conversational lull.

Betty and Jack exchanged a look. "We don't have to be back for work until after the New Year," Betty said.

"We actually wanted to talk to you about that," Jack added.

Her nerves suddenly tightened. "Oh?"

"Erin tells us you've left your job at that bookstore here in Billings to spend some time in Thunder Canyon with your mother and brother."

"I'm not sure if that's a permanent leave or not. I guess you could say I'm on sabbatical."

Jack and Betty exchanged another look, then Betty reached across the table and gripped Elise's hand in hers. Her birth mother's fingers were long and slender, just like hers, Elise thought.

"I know we've mentioned this in passing before but we wanted to make more of a formal offer. We would really love you to come stay with us for a while."

Elise felt a lump rise in her throat at their hopeful faces and she didn't know how to respond.

Betty squeezed her fingers. "We have tons of room now. It's just the two of us, since your brothers…" She faltered a little and looked at Jack for help, then cleared her throat. "Since our sons are both back east now."

Elise had never lived anywhere but Montana. The idea of moving to California wasn't without some appeal, she had to admit, but beneath the table, Matt's long leg tensed next to hers and a muscle flexed in his jaw—reminding her of a very big reason she wasn't sure she wanted to leave Montana just now.

The Castros seemed to sense her hesitation.

"Don't worry about answering now," Jack said in that gruff tone she was beginning to recognize was characteristic for him when his emotions were involved. "You just think about it over the holidays. And you know, maybe you might enjoy just coming down for a couple weeks and testing the waters a bit."

"Which are lovely, by the way," Betty added. "The waters, I mean. Beach, sunshine, perfect weather."

"Beats scraping six inches of snow off your car every morning during a Montana winter," Jack said.

"I can see where it would." She managed a smile, more than a little charmed by this taciturn police officer.

She thought of her father, strong and honorable and handsome, always willing to listen to her troubles and offer her advice. She had desperately missed having a father in her life during her formative teenage years, when everything from boys to school to her future seemed so confusing. Grant had tried to fill a paternal role in her life, but an older brother's advice wasn't quite the same as a father's.

"I'll think about it," she promised them now, aware of Matt's continued tension beside her.

The conversation shifted to foods she enjoyed and stories about her childhood. By the time they finished dessert, some of the tautness in her shoulders had eased.

She was suddenly glad she had come—and immensely grateful to Matt for being so willing to step up and join them as her support system.

"Thank you for coming all the way to Billings just for dinner," Jack said after he'd picked up the check. "We would have been happy to come to Thunder Canyon, you know. We're going to be there anyway in a few days."

"I know. That's what Betty said when we discussed arrangements over the phone. But I really didn't mind coming here."

Actually, she had been the one to suggest they meet in Billings—she just hadn't told the Castros why—that she wanted to avoid all the prying eyes in Thunder Canyon and those who would be sure to gossip about Elise meeting up with her birth parents for dinner.

Since the Castros mentioned they planned to stay with friends in Billings before coming to Thunder Canyon in time for Christmas, she had jumped at the opportunity to meet them in relatively neutral territory.

"This was lovely," Betty said while they were finding their coats.

"It was." Elise shivered a little when Matt's fingers brushed her hair as he helped her into her coat.

"We'll see you again while we're here," Betty said. "Your mother invited us out to the ranch for Christmas Eve, then called back to say you were all going to a big party at some new lodge and we were invited to that as well."

Helen hadn't mentioned she had invited the Castros to Connor McFarlane's lodge opening.

"Everyone in town is talking about it," Elise said. "Matt and his father actually built it."

"It will be good to see some of our old Thunder Canyon friends," Jack said.

A few hours ago, Elise might have dreaded the idea of facing them again in a few days. Now she didn't find it nearly as overwhelming. She was making progress, she thought. Baby steps still made up forward motion, right?

"Have a safe journey back to town, my dear," Betty said. She wrapped Elise in a lavender-scented hug. When she pulled away, Elise was disconcerted to see tears in her eyes. She was more surprised when Jack also wrapped his arms around her.

"You think about what we said, about coming down to San Diego. We would sure love having you there."

"I will," she promised.

Matt took her hand when they left the restaurant. The sky was a starless matte black and the air carried the smell of impending snow.

Matt held the door of his pickup open for her. Acting completely on impulse, Elise brushed her lips along his jawline. "Thank you so much for coming with me tonight. It means the world to me. I'm not sure I could have made it through without you."

He shook his head and kissed her forehead. "You did fine, El. Great, in fact. I could barely tell you were nervous."

She eased back onto the seat while he walked around to the driver's side. When he climbed inside and started the truck, he immediately turned the heater on high to take away the chill.

"They seem like nice people," he said.

"They are." She closed her eyes and rotated her neck to ease some of the strain of the evening. "I think I suddenly realized tonight that letting them into my life and maybe my heart isn't really a betrayal of my family."

He gripped her fingers in his. "Of course it's not. There's room enough in there for everybody."

Including tall, dark-eyed cowboys with sexy smiles.

Elise shivered a little, suddenly stunned by how very quickly Matt had become such an important part of her life.

Despite the poor timing and the general emotional uproar in her life, she was falling in love with him. Real love, not some girlish infatuation. Each moment she spent with him, those ties binding her heart to him tugged a little more tightly.

She ought to be terrified, but somehow all she could manage for now was a little flare of panic, quickly squelched.

"I hate to ask after you've already been so wonderful to come all this way with me just for a steak…"

"A great steak. And wonderful company," he corrected.

She smiled. "Right. But I forgot one of my mother's Christmas presents at our house here in Billings. I bought it months ago and hid it in the back of the closet. Somehow I overlooked it when I was packing for the move to Thunder Canyon. The house is only a few blocks from here. Do you mind if we stop there before we head back?"

"Not at all."

She gave him directions and a few moments later they drove down the wide, tidy street where she and her mother had lived for more than a decade.

Neighbors along their street had always enthusiastically celebrated the holidays. Every house had decorations of some sort—from a couple of those big inflatable snow globe thingies to the discreet colored bulbs the sweet, elderly Mrs. Hoopes in the little house on the corner left up year-round.

By contrast, the small brick house she shared with her mother looked dark and cheerless against the dank sky, even though a few of the windows gleamed with the lights they had set on timers to avoid announcing to the world the house was empty.

They should have at least put up a Christmas tree before they left for Thunder Canyon. Neither of them had thought of it in all the craziness of discovering the mix-up at Thunder Canyon Hospital twenty-six years ago.

"So do you think you'll go to San Diego with the Castros?" Matt asked after he put the pickup in gear in the driveway of her house.

She shot him a quick look. Though his tone was casual, his brown eyes watched her intently. Her mind flashed back to that stunning kiss beneath the mistletoe, to the soft, tender peace that had wrapped around them like holiday ribbons.

"I need to give it more thought. I certainly wouldn't mind escaping the cold this winter but there are…other reasons I'm not sure I want to leave Thunder Canyon right now."

The silence seemed to seethe between them and she could feel her cheeks burn from more than just the pickup's heater. She reached for the door handle, needing to escape the finely wrought tension inside the cab.

"It should only take me a moment to find the gift in my closet."

"I'll come with you," he said.

"If you want, I'm sure I can find some cocoa or something before we start out back to Thunder Canyon."

"Sounds great."

He opened the door for her then took her elbow to

help her through the snow. She and her mother had paid a neighbor boy to keep the walks clear and it looked as if he was keeping up with his responsibility. Still, Matt didn't let go and she was grateful for his warmth as he helped her up the steps to the small porch.

Inside, the house had that expectant feeling of a place that hadn't seen human interaction in a few weeks. The air was musty and still and a thin layer of dust that would make her mother crazy if she saw it had already begun to settle on everything.

Matt flipped on more lights, taking an obvious interest in the comfortable chic decor Helen favored.

Though small, the house had always seemed warm and bright to Elise, especially after the oppressive darkness that had descended on Clifton's Pride after her father's murder.

"Nice," Matt said.

She smiled as she untwisted her scarf and set it on the usual spot atop the console table in the entry.

"I think it became a haven of sorts for both of us after my father died. Grant was busy with his own life by then, so my mother and I just had each other. We made a pretty good life here."

"You didn't want to go off on your own?"

She shrugged. "I moved into an apartment for a year or so while I was in college but it seemed silly to pay rent when my mother and I have always had a great relationship and never seemed to get in each other's way."

She paused and gestured to the living room. "Go ahead and make yourself comfortable. It will only take me a minute to grab my mom's present and then I'll see what I've got in the kitchen."

"Why don't I do a walk-through of the house, check the pilot lights on the furnace and water heater, the pipes, that sort of thing?"

She smiled a little. Wasn't that just like him, to think about those sorts of guy details that probably wouldn't have occurred to her? "Thanks. Good thinking," she answered, then headed down the hall to her bedroom.

Her room was icy and she took a moment to flip on the gas fireplace for an instant warm-up. After she pulled her desk chair over to her closet, she climbed up to dig in the back recesses of her top shelf for the handcrafted necklace and earring set she had purchased for her mother at a summer art fair and then promptly forgotten about until the other day.

After she returned the chair to her desk, her gaze landed on a framed picture that had sat there so long it had become a usually overlooked part of the landscape.

She picked it up, the glass frame cold and heavy in her hands. The picture had been taken at Clifton's Pride a few weeks before her father's death. If she remembered correctly, one of her aunts had taken it near the horse paddock and it featured all of them—John, Helen, Grant and her, looking skinny and small with blond braids and a little freckled nose.

She looked absolutely nothing like the rest of her family. Everything was different—the shape of her eyes, the tilt of her nose. How had they all missed the signs for all these years?

She was a changeling, an interloper.

Her thumb traced John Clifton's strong, smiling features, frozen forever in her memory just like this. Raw emotions bubbled up in her throat, clogging her breath. She missed him so dearly.

What would he have to say about this whole mess? She couldn't even begin to guess. Then she thought of Jack Castro and his gruff eagerness to be part of her life.

It was too much. The stress of the evening, her conflicted feelings, everything. She sagged onto her desk chair and clutched the photograph to her chest, fighting tears and memories and this gaping sense of loss.

Some time later, she heard Matt walking down the hall and hurriedly swiped at her stupid tears.

"Everything looks like it's running just fine," he said. "I nudged the thermostat up a little bit while we're here. Remind me to turn it back down when we go."

His voice trailed off as he entered the room and Elise winced. Why did he always have to see her at her worst? She felt like she had been an emotional mess since the moment she bumped into him at The Hitching Post.

He crossed to her quickly, his eyes dark with concern. "What's the matter? What happened?"

She gave a resigned sigh and held out the picture. "I thought I was doing so much better about everything tonight at dinner. Coming to terms with…all of it. I had a good time with Jack and Betty. They're very nice people, people I think I could grow to care about. Then I saw this picture of my family…the family I've always known as mine…and I just feel like I've lost something somehow."

"Oh, sweetheart. Come here."

He pulled her into his arms and she hitched in a breath, feeling foolish and weepy and deeply grateful.

"This is so stupid." She sniffled. "I'm such a mess."

"Anyone else would be in the same situation. You've had the rug yanked out from under you again, just like it was when your father was killed."

She stared at him, stunned that he could so clearly understand something she hadn't even put together in her own head. She felt as if she were reliving those terrible days of loss and uncertainty all over again. "That's it exactly! I'm not sure how to go on now that everything has suddenly changed."

"You're doing fine, Elise. Give yourself some credit."

His faith in her warmed a cold place deep inside. "Thanks, Matt. You must be so sick of me and my maunderings.

Yes. Exactly! She felt as if she were reliving those terrible days of loss and uncertainty all over again as she struggled to adapt to her changing situation.

"I don't know what that word means," he admitted with a soft smile. "But I'm not sick of you. I could never be sick of you, Elise."

His arms tightened around her and with a sense of inevitability, she lifted her mouth to his. When his lips slanted over hers lightly, the whole twisting, crazy emotional snarl inside her seemed to settle.

The kiss was slow and tender, and she closed her eyes and savored it.

"Thank you," she murmured after a long moment. "I don't know what I would have done without you here tonight, both earlier and just now."

"You would have made it through," he replied. "You're much tougher than you seem to think, El."

"When you say that, you make me want to believe it."

He kissed her, his arms a warm comfort around her. "I remember after your dad died, watching how you coped with everything you'd been hit with. I thought then what a strong person you were. I could tell you were hurting, but you survived it. I always admired that about you."

She was quiet for a long moment, her feelings for him a thick, solid weight in her chest, and then she stood on tiptoe again and kissed him, telling him with her mouth and her hands the feelings she was afraid to voice.

He pulled her against him and deepened the kiss and they stood wrapped together for long moments while the flame from her gas fireplace flickered and danced and tiny snow pellets hissed against the windows.

She wanted to be with him. The yearning blossomed inside her, fierce and powerful. She felt as if everything the last few weeks—okay, for years, if she were honest—had been leading them to this moment.

A low, sultry heat simmered between them and she could taste the change in his kiss, from tenderness to something more, something rich and sensual and delicious.

She pressed against him, tangling her fingers in his hair, stealing sensuous delight through the slide of her tongue along his.

He made no move to capitalize on the convenient queen-size bed behind them so Elise decided she would just have to take matters into her own hands. She eased down and pulled him along with her.

He made a low, sexy sound in his throat and stretched along beside her, his body hard and powerful. She could feel the heat of him scorching her, his tightly leashed strength, and for one crazy moment she couldn't believe this was really happening, that she was really here with Matt Cates.

Somewhere in her room amid the collected detritus of her childhood—maybe in a box of keepsakes under her bed?—was the diary she'd kept in elementary and junior high school, where she had poured out all her silly angst about him.

Why wouldn't he notice her?

He sat with that silly, brainless Jamie Fletcher at lunchtime.

He smiled and joked with her while they were standing in line for the drinking fountain.

She wondered how he would react if he knew about her girlhood crush. Would he be mortified or amused?

She didn't care. Not right now, with his arms around her. This was so much more wonderful than anything she could have imagined back then.

His mouth trailed down her throat, his breath warm on her skin. Everything inside her seemed to sigh. If she had even an inkling back then how magical kissing Matt could be, she would have gladly tripped through the hallway every single day at school, if that was the only way to make him notice her.

His mouth slid just below the loose cowl of her sweater, and she shivered, aching for his touch.

"We'd probably better stop," he murmured.

"Why?"

His gaze met hers, clear reluctance there. "We've still got a long drive back to Thunder Canyon tonight."

"It's snowing," she pointed out in what she thought was a particularly reasonable argument. "Let's just stay here for the night. We can head back in the morning, can't we?"

He sat up and drew in a ragged breath, his eyes dark and hot. "I really don't think that's a great idea, Elise. In case you haven't noticed, I can't seem to keep my hands off you."

She could see his arousal in that slumberous look he wore, hear it in his ragged breathing. He wanted her, just as much as she wanted him, and the realization left her feeling sexy and feminine and powerful.

She hadn't experienced that particular heady mix of emotions very often in her life and she decided to revel in it.

"I don't want you to. Keep your hands off me, I mean. In case *you* haven't noticed, I happen to like your hands on me."

He closed his eyes on a rough-sounding sigh. "Elise—"

"Spend the night here with me, Matt. I want you to."

Chapter Eleven

Her low words sizzled through him, rich and potent, with a hell of a kick. Just like Christmas eggnog. He stared at her, slender and delicate and lovely, and he wanted her with a fierce hunger.

It would be so very easy to take what she was offering, to kiss her and touch her until they were both crazy with need.

But he thought of her tangled emotional state, the stresses weighing on her for the last few weeks and knew he couldn't take advantage of her like that, as much as he ached to taste the passion he sensed brimming just under the surface.

His entire strategy since that night at The Hitching Post had been one of patience. He intended to give her plenty of time to come to terms with everything that had happened the last few weeks with her family—and with the possibility of a deepening relationship between the two of them.

She was throwing that plan all to hell.

He wanted to devour her right now, just cover her body with his, slide beneath that silky-soft comforter on her bed and spend the night wrapped together while the snow clicked against the window and the world outside this room ceased to matter.

He wanted that so intensely he could barely hang on to a coherent thought, but he did his best, knowing this was too important for him to screw it up.

"I'm not sure this is the right time," he began valiantly.

She smiled that soft, reckless smile again and he wondered a little wildly what had happened to his sweet Elise and how this sexy seductress had taken her place.

Not that he was complaining or anything.

"This is the perfect time," she murmured, leaning into him. "I want to be with you. I want it more than I can tell you."

He closed his eyes, praying he could do the right thing here. Finally, he rose and stood beside the bed. When he spoke, his voice was low and tinged with sadness.

"I wish you were saying that because you meant it and not just because you want to forget everything for a little while."

She stared at him for a long moment and then she gave a low, throaty laugh. "Is that what you think this is?"

She rose until only a few inches separated them. He could feel the heat of her, smell the delicious raspberries-and-cream scent. She splayed her fingers against his chest and he could swear she would scorch through the material of his shirt.

"You're wrong, Matt. So wrong. I've wondered how it would be with you since I was old enough to even understand about the difference between men and women. You've never noticed me as anything but sweet little Elise." She sighed. "I guess it's confession time. My thoughts about you have always been anything but sweet."

She smiled again then leaned in to kiss him, her mouth soft and delicious, and he was lost.

This probably wasn't the smartest thing he had ever done but right now he didn't care. The only thing that mattered was Elise and the heartstopping promise of her kiss.

His body was yelling at him to rush, to rip off clothing and surge inside her fast and hard but he drew in a shaky breath and sought control. Not that way, not with Elise—at least not this time.

He felt as if he'd been handed a precious gift all wrapped up in pretty paper, and he wanted to savor every moment of discovering its secrets.

Without lifting his mouth from hers, he lowered them both to the bed again. Her breasts brushed against his chest and her thighs shifted on either side of one of his legs. He propped most of his weight on one elbow, worried a little about crushing her, but she wrapped her arms around him, nestling against him as if she wanted to be nowhere else in the world than right here with him.

"You tell me if you decide you've changed your mind," he ordered against his mouth. "I can't guarantee I'll like it, but I'll stop."

"I can take care of myself, you know," she said with that same enticing smile. "You can stop watching out for me now."

"Never," he said hoarsely.

He deepened the kiss, licking and tasting and exploring her mouth until he couldn't think straight. She tasted so good, sweetly delicious, and he couldn't seem to slake his hunger.

He wanted—needed—more. He slid his fingers beneath her sweater to the small of her back, and his insides trembled at the sensuous contrast of her soft skin against hard, calloused fingers that had driven a few too many nails.

"My hands are too rough," he murmured. "I don't want to hurt you."

"Never," she repeated his words earlier and eased into his touch.

They kissed for a long time, until she sat up a little and reached to pull the edges of her sweater over her head, leaving her in only a lacy red bra that barely cupped her lush little breasts and instantly ratcheted his temperature up about a thousand degrees.

He gulped. "Um. Wow."

She laughed. "I like sexy lingerie. It's a quirk, I know. I guess you'll just have to decide if you can accept it."

"It's going to be tough," he growled, "but I can probably manage."

He unbuttoned his own shirt and pulled it off, aware of her eyes watching every moment and the hot tendrils of hunger coiling through him. He knew he'd been attracted to her before, but he never expected this sort of wild, ferocious heat.

She spread a hand over his chest and made a sexy little sound in her throat and then she toppled him backward on the bed and kissed him, her honey-blond hair a silky, sensuous veil around them.

How the hell had he overlooked her all these years? What was he thinking, always considering her just a sweet kid he needed to watch out for? A smart guy would have seen the sexy woman inside all that sweetness and would have jumped at any chance to be with her like this much sooner. He felt like he'd wasted far too much time as it was and didn't want to squander another moment.

She was everything he had ever wanted, all those nebulous things he hadn't admitted, even to himself. Even as they kissed and touched, he was aware of that edge of uncertainty around them. Her life was in chaos right now—as she'd said, she wasn't in a good place for a relationship. Though he knew it would be difficult, especially after tonight, he would just have to dig deep for patience.

He could wait. For now he had this, he had her, and he wasn't about to waste time worrying about all those uncertainties.

He slid his hands to the sides of her breasts above

the lace of her bra and she hitched in a breath, her stomach muscles contracting. "Oh, yes. Perfect," she murmured.

"Not yet," he said with a lopsided grin. "But heading there."

He was wrong. This was sheer heaven.

Elise felt powerful, sensual. He carefully flipped her back onto the pillow and danced his thumbs over her curves, then pushed one of her bra cups away before lowering his mouth.

She gasped aloud and gripped his head tightly, arching against him and holding him in place while he tasted and explored one and then the other.

With one hand, she slid her fingers through his hair, with the other she explored all that tantalizing skin stretched across his strong back.

The years of construction work had hardened him. He wasn't bulky but every inch was tightly leashed muscle and she wanted to taste all of it. She pressed a kiss to the muscles that corded between his neck and his shoulder and knew the exultant power of feeling his tremble of reaction.

Despite the fact that he was here, in her arms, in her bed, this still didn't seem real. She was afraid she would wake up and he would be gone.

She was almost more afraid that she would wake up and he would be right here, all those hard muscles and tender concern shoving their way into her defenseless heart.

"I care about you, Elise," Matt murmured after they

had removed the rest of their clothing, after their bodies were entwined and all that hard strength surrounded her. "I want you to know, this is important to me. *You're* important to me."

His words seemed to sneak through whatever was left of her paltry defenses to nestle in next to her heart. As much as they scared her, in a weird sort of way they managed to calm her more.

She *was* in love with him. This wasn't infatuation or friendship with benefits but something she had never known before.

Maybe that's why she had been fighting her feelings so hard. She wasn't sure she was strong enough to survive the sort of heartache Matt could leave behind.

She thought of Grant and Stephanie, how deeply they loved each other. They only had to walk into a room together and you could feel it snap in the air like ions whirling just before an electrical storm.

Marlon and Haley shared the same sort of love and everyone could see it.

She supposed she had always expected that when she finally fell in love it would be a soft and easy sort of thing, like settling in near the fireplace with a good book—even as some part of her had yearned for exactly this sort of wild, consuming passion.

"You're important to me, too," she confessed, her voice low. She wasn't going to worry about heartbreak. Not now. For now, she only wanted to focus on this moment, this man, the incredible heat and wonder of being in his arms.

He gripped her hands in his and kissed her as he

entered her with one powerful surge. Oh, yes. Now it was perfect. Her body shifted and settled to accommodate him and she wanted to lie here beneath him for the next week or two, just savoring this rare and beautiful connection between them.

"Elise," he murmured. "My sweet Elise."

She loved the sound of her name spoken in that rough-edged voice, the heat in his eyes as he kissed her.

She clutched his back as he surged inside her, every muscle shivering with delight. She felt as if she were like that eagle in the needlepoint they had bought for Haley, as if she were soaring and circling on currents of air with widespread wings, climbing higher and higher toward the sun. And then he kissed her, his mouth fierce and demanding, and reached a hand between their bodies, to the heat and ache at her core, and she climaxed in one mad, crazy instant that left her gasping and arching against him needing more and more.

When she glided back to earth, she found him watching her out of those hot, hungry, dark eyes.

"That was just about the sexiest thing I've ever seen," he said on a growl, then he kissed her fiercely and she held him while he found his own release.

After he had taken care of the condom—even in this, he protected her—Matt slid back into bed and pulled her close, nestling her against all his heat and strength. "You matter to me," he said again.

The snow continued to beat against the window and the sky looked dark and menacing, but here they were safe together. With her cheek resting on his chest, she listened to his strong, steady heartbeat in her ear and thought about love and fear, fantasy and reality and the strange twistings of fate, until she fell asleep.

For the first time in his life, Matt found himself reluctant to return to Thunder Canyon.

Usually he loved driving through town, that first glimpse of the mountains, the sense of homecoming, of belonging in a beautiful place.

Not today. Climbing out of Elise's bed in the predawn hours was just about the hardest thing he ever had to do. Unfortunately, though he would like to forget everything and stay right here, he had obligations waiting for him, the last few finishing details to the McFarlane Lodge, and knew they needed to make an early start.

Okay, he hadn't minded the early start—especially when he woke with a soft, sleepy Elise in his arms. She had kissed him, her body warm and pliant, and they had pleasured each other while dawn stretched across the sky.

He would have liked to think the incredible night and morning they spent in each other's arms could magically solve all the issues between them.

Unfortunately, reality wasn't always so cooperative. With each mile that he drove closer to Thunder Canyon, she seemed to pull away from him, until it was all he could do not to jerk the pickup around and head back to Billings.

Though she continued to make small talk with him— about the weather, about the Christmas gifts she was giving her family, about the things she had enjoyed at her job at the bookstore—she seemed distant, distracted.

Her words would sometimes trail off in the middle of a sentence and he would shift his attention from the road for a moment, to find her gazing absently out the window.

Finally, when they were only a mile outside the Thunder Canyon town boundaries, he knew he had to do something to try yanking her back toward him.

"Connor McFarlane's lodge is nearly finished," he said. "We should be wrapping it up today."

"I've heard it's beautiful. Haley said your dad gave her a tour and she can't stop talking about all the luxurious details."

"McFarlane's throwing a big party on Christmas Eve, inviting most of the town."

"Yes. My mother and Grant are planning on going. Remember, the Castros said they were going, too."

"That's right. I forgot we talked about it last night at dinner." He grabbed her hand and squeezed her fingers. "I guess I've been a little distracted."

He loved watching that little blush steal over her features. He had a feeling he would never tire of it.

"You and your father should certainly be the guests of honor for all the hard work you've put into the place."

He shrugged. "Like you said about the ROOTS party the other night, it was a team effort. But watching people enjoy a place you've built is a gratifying experience."

His hands tightened on the steering wheel. Nerves curled in his gut, something that didn't sit well with him.

"Listen, I want to take a date to the party. Specifically, you."

Her eyes widened and he didn't miss the barely perceptible clenching of her fingers in his.

"Matt, I'm not sure I'm ready for that."

He gave her a long look across the width of the cab. "Funny. I would have thought last night proved you were."

She sighed. "Everyone in town is already whispering that I'm the reason you broke your engagement to Christine. Yesterday morning before you and I left for Billings, I went to the grocery store with Steph and three people stopped her to ask if it was true the wedding was off. None of them would meet my gaze and I could practically feel the disapproval radiating off them. The two of us showing up together at the McFarlane Christmas party would certainly add considerable fuel to that rumor."

There she went, trying to find excuses again. Just how hard was a guy supposed to work before he gave a cause up as lost?

He thought about the connection they had forged together the night before, the sweet peace they had shared, and he was angry, suddenly, that she seemed willing to give that up without a fight.

"Who the hell cares about a little gossip? You and I both know it's not true and so does Christine. What else matters?"

She huffed out a breath. "That's easy for you to say. You've never cared about gossip. Good grief, you and

Marlon spent your lifetime raising as much trouble as you could, gossip be hanged."

He acknowledged some truth to that, but those days seemed far away.

"I'm not like you," she went on. "I hate finding myself the center of attention—and I feel like I haven't been standing anywhere else since the day Erin Castro showed up in Thunder Canyon."

She paused and pulled her fingers away from his. "When my father was murdered, I know everyone talked about me all the time. I could feel the conversation stop. Nobody talked to me about his murder except my few close friends. Haley, mostly, since Steph was in a pretty dark place with her dad's murder, too."

She sighed. "With everyone else, I felt like I had entered some kind of social black hole. I know they were kids and probably didn't have the skills to deal with such a rough thing. Nobody knew what to say, I guess, so it was easier to ignore me. But it still hurt, especially because I know everyone said plenty behind my back."

"I always talked to you," he said curtly, sick of her excuses and the whole damn situation. "*Always.* And I never let anybody say anything hurtful about you or your family, at least when I was in earshot."

He could feel her gaze on him. He shifted his attention from the road long enough to see her features soften. She reached a hand out and touched his thigh.

"You always did," she agreed. "You've been riding to my rescue since we were kids, haven't you?"

He couldn't have this conversation while he was

driving, he decided. Since they were close to Clifton's Pride, he steered onto the shoulder and put the truck in gear so he could safely face her.

"Because I care about you, Elise. I always have. I convinced myself you were just a sweet girl, maybe a little naive, who needed somebody to watch her back. And then you showed up in town again and I realized my feelings for you ran much, much deeper."

She drew in a shaky breath. "I care about you, too, Matt. Last night was…well, you know what it was. I don't want to screw this up. But I don't have the greatest track record with relationships and I'm so afraid."

"You think I'm not? You scare the hell out of me, Elise."

She gazed out the window at a magpie scavenging for berries on the stark, bare crimson dogwood branches along the ice-crusted creek. "I'm not bringing my best self to this," she finally said. "I don't think I can right now."

Those nerves in his gut coiled more tightly. "So instead of giving me the chance to show you I can be patient, you want to push me away, just as you've been doing since you came back to town."

"I don't know. Maybe." She sighed. "I told you I was a mess, Matt."

"I guess you have to decide what's more important to you. A little pointless gossip." He took a chance and reached for her hand, then drew her cool fingers to his mouth. "Or the way we feel about each other."

She narrowed her gaze at him. "Not fair."

He grinned and put the pickup in gear to drive the

rest of the way to the ranch house. "Whoever said I was fair?"

When they reached Clifton's Pride, he could already see a few signs of life, though the day was just starting: A ranch hand hauling a bucket of something, a light on in the kitchen, the rumble of a tractor probably hauling hay bales out to hungry cattle in some distant, snow-covered pasture.

He moved around to open her door before she could climb out and helped her down from the high truck. "I'll swing by before the party. I really hope you'll be here."

She sighed. "You're not going to give up, are you?"

"I walked away from law school without a backward look and haven't regretted it for a moment. But something tells me if I gave up on you as easily as I did that, it would haunt me for the rest of my life."

Chapter Twelve

"Here we go."

Matt parked his pickup in front of the sprawling Mc-Farlane Lodge and Elise could do nothing but stare.

"Wow! It's gorgeous!"

The house was everything people in town had said, soaring and majestic like the mountains around it. Constructed of log and stone, it seemed part of the landscape, as if it had grown here amid the boulders like the Douglas fir and spruce surrounding it.

"We worked with a log home company out of Helena on the structure but Cates did all the work inside."

"I'm sure it's even more beautiful there than it is from the outside."

"You ready to go see?"

She gazed at Matt across the width of his truck. He

must have showered and shaved just before he picked her up at Clifton's Pride. His brown hair appeared freshly combed, his jaw smooth, and all through the drive here the scent of his sexy soap or aftershave or whatever it was had been driving her crazy.

He wore a dressy black leather bomber-style jacket over a tan twill shirt that made him look rugged and masculine, darkly dangerous.

He looked like the sort of man who could take on dragons. Or at least a house full of curious friends.

"Yes. I think I am."

"I'm really glad you came with me," he said as he opened the door for her.

She had to admit, she had waffled back and forth all week long. Some part of her would have liked to stay back at Clifton's Pride—and not simply because of the potential for wagging tongues.

Since her father's murder, Christmas Eve had become one of her least-favorite days of the year. She didn't miss the irony. Like most kids, she had always loved the holidays when she was a girl. Her father had loved the season, too, and she had many wonderful, vivid memories of her girlhood: Christmas caroling, wrapping gifts, sneaking baskets of gifts and food onto needy porches.

If the weather wasn't too snowy, every Christmas Eve her dad would saddle horses for her and Grant and the three of them would take a long, snowy ride into the mountains while Helen stayed back at the ranch putting the finishing touches to their Christmas Eve dinner.

They were wondrous times for a girl, filled with

laughter and excitement and breathless anticipation. After his death, all the joy and magic of the holidays seemed to die with him. Helen had tried to make an effort, but over the years Elise had come to the point where she wanted to just forget the whole day.

She'd even come to dread it, finding it too much of a struggle to pretend to be bright and cheerful when she wasn't.

As they walked up the winding pathway to the house, Elise tried to tamp down her nerves. She was so tired of this wild tangle of emotions. She wanted to just enjoy herself today, to focus on family and friends.

And Matt, the man who had become so very important to her.

Now, on the porch of the home he had built, she looked around at the fine-crafted details. The outdoor lighting looked like something out of a museum and the massive front door was hand-carved, a sculpted, twisted design of a tree with curving branches.

She couldn't resist touching the polished wood. "Wow. This is really exquisite, Matt. Beyond anything I expected."

He looked pleased at her praise and that fragile tenderness fluttered in her chest.

She had missed him this week. Both of them had been preoccupied with family obligations and he was busy with the beginning stages of a new Cates Construction project. She had only seen him once, when he had picked her up two nights earlier for a quiet dinner at his house.

Afterward, they had bundled up and gone for a chilly

walk through the darkened streets of town with his chocolate Lab bounding through the snowdrifts ahead of them. Though they didn't encounter a moose this time as they had in Bozeman, walking hand in hand through the snowy streets in the moonlight had been sweet and peaceful.

He had kissed her when he took her back to Clifton's Pride but not with the heat and passion she wanted. Rather, he had exhibited remarkable—albeit frustrating—restraint and had limited their embrace to a few brief moments.

She pulled her fingers away from the door and slipped them through his. "It's really stunning, Matt. I'm very impressed."

"Come and see the rest."

He pushed open the door and they were instantly assaulted by noise—shrieking children, jazzy holiday music playing through hidden speakers, laughter and the low, chattering hum of a dozen conversations.

She knew just about everyone. Her mother was talking with Steph's mother and Judy Johnson, owner of the Clip N' Curl. In another seating group, she spied Holly Clifton talking with Erika and Shandie Traub.

A few people looked up at their entrance and Elise thought she saw a few raised eyebrows, but she told herself she didn't care. Matt was right, a little gossip wouldn't hurt her.

They hadn't made it two steps inside when suddenly Christine Mayhew hurried over to them, her arms outstretched. To Elise's shock, Christine pulled her into a warm hug, laughing and talking about something one of the children had just said. She hugged Matt next and then looped an arm through Elise's.

Elise saw confusion on more than a few faces. She was confused, too, since she had barely met Christine but the woman was acting as if they were best friends.

Christine talked with them for several moments before excusing herself. "There's Tori. I need to ask her who did that incredible oil painting in the master bedroom."

Before she walked away, she gave Matt a sidelong smile. "Unless you think that wasn't sufficient to prove to everyone in town you didn't wrench out my poor little heart and drive over it with your backhoe, you beast."

He grinned. "That ought to do it. Thanks, Chris."

"Anytime," she said with another hug to Elise before she sauntered away.

"So that was all a setup?" Elise asked.

He shrugged, trying and failing to look innocent. "I figured the best way to shut off the gossip valve in a hurry was to show that this is not some torrid love triangle. Looks like it worked."

Oh, she was in serious trouble. That tenderness zinged through her again and she was immeasurably touched that he would make the effort to keep her out of the spotlight.

She should have expected it. He *was* her self-appointed protector, wasn't he? Apparently that covered everything from schoolyard bullies to social scandals.

She couldn't resist smiling at him. "You're a very sweet man, Matt," she murmured.

His brown-eyed gaze met hers and everything inside

her sighed at the warm light there. "Guys don't like to be called sweet, El," he said with a mock growl.

She checked to make sure they were out of earshot of others at the party, then she spoke in a voice pitched low so only he could hear. "Okay. How about this. When you do thoughtful little things like that, I find it incredibly sexy. Even better than that thing you do with your tongue in my ear."

He gave a rough laugh. "Cut it out or I'll be dragging you out of the party before we even say hello to our hosts."

As much as the idea of that appealed to her right now, she knew this party was important to him. He had worked hard to create a showplace for Connor McFarlane and was justified in being pleased with his efforts.

"I want to see the house. Will you give me a private tour? Show me all the secret corners and out-of-the-way closets?"

He sent her a dark look but grabbed her hand and led her up the staircase. On the way, he pointed out details like the hand-peeled banister and the imported light fixtures.

He kept up a running commentary as he led her from room to room. Though she wouldn't have thought she could find a discussion on the challenges of post-and-beam construction fascinating, he made it interesting and she admired the obvious care Cates Construction had put into the work.

In one of the bedrooms, he started discussing the relative merits of using alder or black walnut. He was so impassioned about it, she couldn't help herself, she wrapped her arms around his neck and pulled his mouth down to hers.

For an instant, he only stared at her and then he closed the door firmly, leaning against it so no one could interrupt them while he kissed her properly, as she had been wanting him to do since the moment he picked her up.

That sweet peace fluttered through her as he kissed her, the sense of rightness and home and everything wonderful. She held him close, heat churning through her and her emotions a thick, tangled clog in her throat.

By the time he eased away, both of them were breathing raggedly.

"You're killing me, Elise. Everyone in town is downstairs and all I want to do is lock that door and forget the rest of the world exists. Hell, look at me! I can't even leave this room until I'm a little more…under control."

She glanced down at his obvious arousal and smiled, thoroughly enjoying herself. "Well, then, I guess you'll just have to tell me more about exactly why black walnut is so vastly superior for its hardness and durability."

He stayed a safe distance away for several moments while Elise wandered through the bedroom and its attached bathroom, admiring all the thoughtful little luxuries in the design. Finally, he determined he could face polite company again.

When they left the room and walked down the stairs sometime later, Elise could sense something momentous happening. Excitement seemed to coil through the lodge like the silvery garlands on the tree.

"What's going on?" Matt asked the first people he saw standing at the bottom of the stairway—his brother Mitchell and sister-in-law Lizbeth.

"The craziest thing." Lizbeth's lovely features glowed. "Connor and Tori are getting married."

Matt frowned. "Haven't we all known that for months?"

"No, I mean right now. They decided on the spur of the moment that this was the perfect time to tie the knot, while all their friends and family are already here and everyone is celebrating. We're having a wedding in just a few moments! Won't that just make Christmas Eve perfect?"

"Oh, how wonderful," Elise exclaimed.

"Tori already has her dress and veil. Knowing her fashion sense, it's going to be gorgeous," Lizbeth said.

"What can I do to help?" Elise asked.

"I think everything is nearly ready. Tori's upstairs with Allaire getting dressed. I think Shandie's doing her hair."

"I'll help set up the chairs," Matt said.

For the next half hour the lodge was filled with a flurry of activity as the residents of Thunder Canyon rallied to help organize the last-minute wedding. Flowers and greenery were snatched from the elegant decorations for bouquets and corsages, slim white candles were gathered from various locations around the house and arranged along the mantel and someone shifted the music on the sound system from holiday carols to sweetly romantic songs.

Matt and his brothers and some of the other men

had dragged every available chair into the huge great room and arranged them in rows, all facing the twenty-foot Christmas tree and the sweeping mountain views beyond from the floor-to-ceiling windows.

Now, Elise sat beside him while soft, romantic music played. He reached for her hand as Connor and his teen-age son CJ walked up to stand near the Christmas tree. Connor looked handsome and successful in a gray designer suit that set off his distinctive auburn hair.

Everyone rose when Tori appeared at the top of the curved half timber staircase on the arm of her father, Dr. Sherwood Jones, with her best friend Allaire Traub and CJ's friend Jerilyn Doolin as her attendants.

She looked breathtaking, in an off-the-shoulder, three-quarter-length dress. Shandie had worked wonders with her strawberry-blond hair and it was coiled atop her head in a style both elegant and romantic.

While everyone admired the lovely bride, Elise found her attention shifting to Connor McFarlane, waiting near the windows. Something fragile and sweet tugged in her heart when she witnessed the soft light in his eyes as Tori glided down the stairs with her arm tucked through her father's.

The two of them radiated happiness and Elise wasn't the only one dabbing away tears as she listened to their heartfelt vows and saw their obvious joy in each other.

After the ceremony, Connor brought out magnums of champagne and everyone lifted flutes in a toast to the glowing couple. When several toasts had been offered, Connor nudged Marlon. "You know, we're all set for a wedding now. Everybody's here. Trust me, you could save yourself a lot of trouble if you just took care of things now and tied the knot."

"A lovely offer—thanks," Haley said with a smile. "But I have my heart set on a spring wedding."

"Have you set a date?" Elise asked.

Marlon and Haley exchanged glances. "Yes," Haley answered. "Finally. We decided last night on April 11, if we can put it together that soon."

Tori hugged her. "If we could throw mine together in half an hour, I think a few months should be plenty of time."

"You'll still be my maid of honor, won't you?" Haley asked Elise.

Would she be in Thunder Canyon for the wedding? Elise had no idea what the future held, but she decided she would do whatever it took to help Haley have the most beautiful wedding in Thunder Canyon history. She deserved a wonderful happy ending of her own.

"You couldn't keep me away," she answered with a hug.

"I don't think you're going to be the only ones hearing wedding bells in the near future," Connor said with a gesture toward Erin Castro and Dillon Traub.

They stood in a group with Elise's mother and Grant and Stephanie. Erin and Corey held hands and even from here, Elise could sense the bond between them.

Everyone around her was getting married. She swallowed hard with a careful look at Matt, who had left their group to talk to his father and a few other men.

He looked strong and gorgeous and everything inside her seemed to sigh whenever she saw him. She wanted what it seemed everyone else around them had found but she was so afraid to dream about forever, especially right now when everything felt so topsy-turvy.

Mindful of the hazards of overindulging—hadn't she learned *that* particular lesson painfully well?—she took only a tiny sip of her champagne while she listened to the ebb and flow of conversation around her.

Out of the corner of her gaze, she spied Grant and Stephanie approaching Erin's group. As she watched, her brother slipped an arm around his newly discovered sister's shoulder and guided her to a couple of Thunder Canyon old-timers who must not have had the chance to meet her yet.

The champagne took on a bitter taste and suddenly the room felt close and airless.

Suddenly she thought of what Matt had said the other day, that there was room in her heart for everyone. She was definitely discovering that. She was already coming to care for the Castros. Didn't the same hold true? Just because her family had embraced Erin didn't mean they were pushing her away at the same time.

She let out a shaky breath. She had been acting like a spoiled brat, she realized. She wanted something—her life back, the one she'd known before Erin discovered the hospital mistake. Since she could no longer have it, instead of reacting with dignity and grace and looking for the good in the situation, she felt like she'd been throwing a pissy temper tantrum since Thanksgiving.

How had anybody been able to stand her?

As she gazed out the window, through the trees she saw a wide glimmer of white not far away from

McFarlane Lodge. Silver Stallion Lake, she realized. Because of the way the road curved, she hadn't realized it was so close.

She glanced around the crowded room at everyone celebrating weddings and engagements and Christmas and then looked back at the lake, a favorite spot of locals. The idea of clearing her head was suddenly immensely appealing. Since she didn't think anyone would miss her for a few moments, she headed for the room where they had hung their coats earlier.

A moment later, she slipped out the lovely sculpted door and into the lightly falling snow.

"No, I'm not joking," Bo Clifton, Elise's cousin and the town's new mayor-elect gave Matt's father a solemn look. "Completely serious. I know it's hard to believe but I just got the phone call from the sheriff that they've arrested him."

"Who's under arrest?" Matt asked, overhearing just the tail end of the conversation as he approached them.

"Arthur Swinton," Frank said, eyes wide and shocked.

His father hadn't been a fan of the mayor whom Bo was supposed to be replacing after the new year. He considered him a prosy old windbag, but he seemed as shocked as Matt that the man had been arrested.

"What are the charges?" Matt asked.

"Multiple counts of embezzlement and fraud of public funds," Bo said, his features grim. "You know how the town budget has been struggling so much for the last few years and revenue seems to have dwindled to a trickle? Well, it turns out the soft economy is only partly responsible. Arthur Swinton has been dipping his fat little fingers into the city's coffers, maybe for years."

"I always knew he was difficult to work with," Frank said with disgust. "Always making us jump through ridiculous hoops when it came to building permits and zoning regulations. I just never imagined he was crooked."

"I did," Grant Clifton said. "Everything makes sense now. I never could figure out where the redevelopment tax incentives we'd been promised to expand the resort had disappeared to. Now I know."

"We'll get everything straightened out," Bo promised them all. "I'm pushing hard for the swearing in to be held on New Year's Day so I can start cleaning up this mess and get this town back on track."

Grant clapped him on the shoulder. "Whatever you need, Bo, we'll help. I've been talking with Corey and Dillon Traub and we've got big plans for the resort."

"The Traubs are partnering with Caleb Douglas and Justin Caldwell?" Matt asked, surprised.

"That's the plan," Grant said. "They're looking for another investment and see nothing but good things for Thunder Canyon and the resort in the future. We're talking a major expansion here."

He paused and smiled at the Cateses. "You know, we're going to need a reliable construction company. Cates is at the top of that list."

Pride surged through Matt. His father had built a solid reputation in Thunder Canyon and he knew his work the last few years had only added to that, but his professional satisfaction was tempered by plenty of uncertainty.

Part of him rejoiced at the idea of the revitalization of Thunder Canyon and the role Cates Construction might play in that. But the other part was all tangled up with a woman who didn't even know if she wanted to be anywhere near the town he loved.

News of the mayor's arrest had spread through the party and several people approached Bo for more details. While the man was busy explaining everything he knew about the charges against Swinton, Frank pulled Matt aside.

"You think we can handle a big project like Grant and the Traubs have in mind?" Frank asked. "We might need to add to the crew."

"I'm not sure," Matt admitted.

His father stared. "What do you mean, you're not sure? Wrong answer, son. You're supposed to say, 'Sure, Dad. I got this. We can handle anything.'"

On a professional level, Matt knew the company could handle any challenge that came its way. Hadn't they proved it the last few months by bringing in this job for Connor McFarlane quickly and efficiently?

When it came to his tangled, complicated relationship with Elise, he wasn't sure of anything.

"Dad, I need to be up-front with you," he finally said. "Since we talked last week about me taking over the company, a lot has changed." He paused. "More than a lot. *Everything* has changed."

Concern furrowed his father's brow and Matt squirmed under his scrutiny.

"Let's go where we can talk in private," Frank said gruffly, leading the way through French doors to one of several covered decks off the back of the house.

The deck was warmed by an outdoor gas fireplace, flames dancing and weaving as they pushed away the heavy, expectant cold of an impending storm.

"What do you mean?" Frank said after Matt closed the doors behind him. "What's changed?"

He looked down at the town he loved and was surprised at the ache in his chest. "I might be leaving Thunder Canyon," he said quietly.

Frank stared at him and Matt saw a host of emotions cross those expressive brown eyes, ending with resignation.

"It's Elise Clifton, isn't it?" he asked.

He shoved his hands in his pocket. "How did you... Why would you say that?"

His father shook his head. "I knew the moment I saw you two come in together. You've got that look in your eyes, the one I've seen all three of your brothers wear. Guess I shouldn't be so surprised."

Did he really want to be lumped in with his love-struck brothers? He thought about it for a moment, then gave a slight smile. "Yeah, that about sums it up," he answered.

"Doesn't mean you have to up and leave. Your brothers seem to be happy enough sticking around," Frank said.

"You know I love Thunder Canyon, Dad. If I could figure out a way, I would in a minute. But Elise hasn't been back in a long time. Things here haven't been easy for her. She has some pretty dark memories."

His father was silent for a moment, watching the flakes drift down in the gathering twilight. "She has reason, I suppose. Poor thing. I guess you and she will have to figure out your own path."

"We're working on it. To be honest, it's a hell of a lot more rocky than I expected."

His father nudged him with his shoulder. "The best views always come after a long, hard climb. Don't worry, you'll figure things out. She's not stupid, our Elise."

"Not in the slightest. But she has a lot of things to work through."

"You know your help has been invaluable at the company the last few years," his father said gruffly. "But I'll figure out how to get along without you if I have to."

"Thanks, Dad." He was fiercely grateful, suddenly, for his parents and the support and love they had always showered upon him and his brothers.

"You coming back inside to join the party?" Frank asked.

"In a minute. Think I'll watch the storm come in for a moment."

Sure enough, the snow already seemed a little heavier than it had when they walked onto the deck and those gray-edged clouds looked plump and full.

After his father left, Matt watched the trees twist and curl with the increasing wind. He could see downtown from here, cheerful and bright against the gathering darkness and felt another pang of regret. He would love to live here the rest of his life, to raise children, to help build the town and leave a legacy for those children. He could imagine many more Christmases spent here, filled with joy and laughter, friends and family.

But with something lost, something infinitely more precious could be found.

He was thinking about choices and growth and the future when he spied a slender figure bundled up in a red peacoat heading through the trees. He narrowed his gaze. He knew that coat. He had hung it himself when he and Elise had arrived.

Where was she going? The only thing in the direction of that trail was Silver Stallion Lake.

Of course. Crazy woman. Didn't she know it was dangerous to wander away on her own with that kind of storm brewing? Not to mention, with the above-freezing weather they'd had the last few days, more snow was bound to make the snowpack unstable and avalanche-prone.

All his protective instincts rattled around inside him. No way was he going to stand by while she put herself in possible danger. He hurried back inside the house and found his own coat quickly then headed outside to follow her trail in the gathering gloom.

The trail toward Silver Stallion Lake crossed the narrow road that ended in the box canyon where Connor had built his home. Some distance away toward town, Matt could see a huge cornice of snow blown by the wind now covering the peak at the canyon's edge.

He frowned. Add a few more inches on it and he could easily imagine the danger of a snowslide could potentially be high.

He would have to warn Connor when he returned to the house. But first, he needed to find Elise and make sure she was safe.

He walked quickly through the pines down a deer trail. The snow was soft and light for now and the air smelled of pine and winter. As he expected, he found her at the small lake, surrounded by pines and the pale ghostly skeletons of the winter-bare aspens.

In the few moments' head start she had, she must have unearthed a pair of skates from the small structure on the edge of the lake that was kept stocked with such things for locals' use. She sat on a log bench tying the skate. When she finished, she stood and glided out gracefully onto the ice.

Though he was aware of the need for haste and caution with the storm blowing in, he couldn't resist watching her from his concealed spot in the trees. She looked free and relaxed as she whirled and danced.

He thought of his father's words. He was lovestruck, just as his brothers. The realization should have scared him, sent him hurrying away. Instead, he was aware of a sweet, fragile tenderness.

He loved Elise. No matter what, he loved her. Nothing else mattered. She was everything he had ever wanted, the only thing he needed. If she wanted to move away from Thunder Canyon, he would do it. Hell, he would go live in a hut in Borneo if it meant he could have Elise with him.

He finally emerged from the trees and made his way down the trail toward the bank of the frozen lake.

She toed to a stop when she spotted him and stood waiting as he carefully moved across the ice.

A thin trail of tears had left a mark down her cheeks and his heart ached for her. "Oh, sweetheart. Are you okay?" he asked.

She smiled and it took a few beats for him to realize what seemed so different about her. Despite the tear stains, she looked relaxed, happy.

At peace.

"My dad used to bring me to the lake all the time when I was a little girl. I had completely forgotten how much I love it here. It always seemed to me when I was little that the mountains appear to cup this valley like comforting hands. That sounds silly, doesn't it?"

"Not to me."

"I can see my dad clear as day, holding my hands and towing me along the ice while I slipped and slid and tried to find my skate legs for the first few moments. I wasn't the most graceful kid, as you might recall. I was so clumsy everywhere else but when I skated, it seemed like I forgot that."

He pictured her as a little girl, small and slender for her age, running so fast she often stumbled as she tried to keep up with all the other kids. He could visualize her father, too, strong and handsome, a man everyone in town had admired and respected.

Learning she wasn't genetically John Clifton's child must feel to her as if she had lost her father all over again. He couldn't even imagine how difficult it must be for her.

He wanted to comfort her, to say something magical

that would make her pain disappear. He couldn't think of any words so he reached out and gripped her mittens in his own gloves.

"Is this the way he did it?" he asked and began walking backward, pulling her across the ice.

"Be careful. You're going to fall," she warned.

His heart was a sweet, heavy ache in his chest. "I'm counting on you to catch me, Elise."

Her gaze locked with his, emotions churning there. Despite the party still in full swing back at the McFarlane Lodge, despite the storm hovering just out of view, despite all the turmoil, he wouldn't have traded this moment for anything.

Just the two of them in the quiet hush of a miraculous Christmas Eve.

After a few passes across the lake, he stopped in the middle of the ice and with a sense of destiny, he pulled her into his arms and kissed her.

Her mouth was cold against his but she sighed and wrapped her mittened hands around his waist, leaning into him.

The kiss was slow and lovely. Perfect for the evening and the moment.

"You should know something," he murmured against her mouth. "I told my dad just now that I might not be taking over Cates Construction after all."

She eased away from him, her expression perplexed. "Why? I thought you loved being a builder. Are you thinking of going back to law school?"

"No. I do love the work. But I figured I can do the

same thing anywhere. Billings. Bozeman. Even San Diego if that's where you decide you want to go."

He brushed his mouth over hers. His heart seemed to pound loudly in his ears. This was a risk he had never taken with a woman before—never *wanted* to take. With her, it was right. He knew it deep in his bones.

"I love you, Elise," he murmured.

She drew away from him sharply and nearly stumbled backward on the ice. Her hands flailed a little before she caught her balance. "You...what?"

He saw shock and disbelief and something else, a tiny spark of something bright and joyful that filled him with hope.

"I love you," he repeated firmly. "If you're not happy in Thunder Canyon because of the memories or your dad or what's happened with your family or whatever, I won't try to convince you to stay. I would never do that to you."

He moved forward to take her hands in his again while the fat flakes landed in her lashes, on her cheeks, in her hair. He pulled her across the ice into his arms again and kissed the corner of her mouth.

"You don't have to stay in Thunder Canyon, Elise. But I'm not about to let you go somewhere else without me."

She closed her eyes for a long moment. When she opened them, that tiny sliver of hope he had seen had been replaced by sadness.

"You can't love me, Matt."

"Why not?"

She didn't answer, only pulled her hands away from him and headed across the ice, her movements no longer full of grace and beauty but abrupt, forceful, each stroke digging into the ice.

He followed after her as she sat down on the log to remove the ice skates. "Don't tell me how I feel, Elise. I've never been in love before but I know exactly what this is. I'm crazy about you."

"How can you be?" she asked, her voice bitter. "I'm such a mess and you seem to have borne the brunt of it these last few weeks."

He heard the despair in her voice, that sadness that had seemed such a part of her since she had come back.

But he had also seen that moment of joy in her eyes. He had tasted the heat of her kiss and sensed the suppressed emotions behind it.

She cared about him. They had something special here and he wasn't about to let her throw it away because of some misguided idea that she didn't belong here.

If he ever thought he might have had the skills to be persuasive in a courtroom, now would probably be a really good time to prove it.

He sat beside her on the fallen log, remembering when he and some buddies had dragged it over to the edge of the lake a few years back.

"You asked me how I can love you," he said quietly. "A better question would be, how can I not? Yes, you've had a rough few weeks. But no matter what you think, all I've seen is a woman facing a hard situation with strength and courage."

She flashed him a look, then returned to unlacing her skate. He hoped she was listening. All he could do was try.

"Despite your own turmoil," he went on, "you've reached out to everyone else in town. Just look at what you did for Haley last week and how hard you worked to make Christmas great for some needy kids at ROOTS, despite your own ambivalence about the holidays?"

"Haley's my friend. I did it to help her."

"I saw you with all those kids, Elise. You can tell yourself you were only helping Haley but I saw how excited you were to give them all their gift bags—the bags you spent hours preparing. And the Castros. You were so great with them at dinner, patiently answering all their questions about your childhood even though I saw how difficult it was for you to be there."

"You helped me get through that. I'm not sure I could have done it on my own."

"You could have," he assured her. "But don't you think it's significant that you asked me to come with you? That you turned to me for help when you needed it?"

He reached for her hand and brought it to his mouth. "I love you, Elise. No matter how much you've been fighting it, I know you have feelings for me, too. I want a future with you, no matter where and what shape that future might take."

Chapter Thirteen

Elise listened to his words, low and fervent amid the snowflakes fluttering down, and that tiny, fragile joy curled through her again.

This couldn't be real. She couldn't really be sitting on the banks of Silver Stallion Lake with Matt Cates declaring his love for her. Things like this didn't happen to girls next door like her. Any moment now, she was going to wake up and discover this was only some surreal dream brought on by too much eggnog.

But now, if it were a dream, she wouldn't feel the wet snow in her hair, the cold of the ice seeping through her boots.

"I love you, Elise," Matt murmured one more time. "You trusted me out on that ice not to let you fall, just as I trusted you. Don't you think we can trust each other about this?"

She stared at him as the snow fell heavier, until his features were hazy, indistinct.

She didn't need to see him. She knew every line, every angle of his face.

She loved him.

The precious truth of it slid through her, filling and healing every battered aching corner of her heart.

She loved him—and she suddenly knew that if she threw this chance away, she would be the craziest woman who had ever come out of Thunder Canyon.

She gave a tiny, bubbling little laugh, unable to contain so much happiness inside.

"You're right. You're so very right."

"Elise—"

"I love you, Matt. I have loved you most of my life, if you want the truth. Those days when we were in school and you were always watching out for me, keeping me safe—you were my hero, Matt. Everything I ever dreamed about."

He made a low sound of disbelief and for some reason, that made her laugh again. She was so happy, she wanted to shout it to the trees, to spin around and around on the ice like she was a fearless, clumsy six-year-old again.

She took off her mittens then reached for his hands and slid his glove off so she could raise his warm hand to her cold cheek.

She held his hand there against her skin. "I had no

idea back then how you would ride to my rescue again, Matt. You saved me."

"No, I didn't. You would have come through."

"Maybe. But I feel like I was falling through that ice, floundering in the cold, and you reached a hand in and yanked me back to light and warmth again. Thank you for that and for…giving me back myself."

She smiled tremulously. "I love you."

He stared at her and she saw heat and wonder and she thought she might even see the sheen of tears there. "Are you sure you don't have dreams of being an attorney? That's quite a closing argument."

"No, thank you." She smiled.

He kissed her there amid the falling snow and she tasted a sweet tenderness and the promise of a beautiful future.

Her father would have approved, she thought. He would have been delighted she found someone who could make her so very happy, who could pick her up when she stumbled, brush her off, and give her a chance to soar across life like she skated across Silver Stallion Lake.

They kissed softly for a long time, love wrapping them tightly together against the elements.

Finally, he drew away from her. "We're going to freeze to death if we stay here much longer. Do you think you're ready to go back?"

She slid her hand into his, loving his heat and the solid strength of him. "No," she answered. "But I think I'm ready to go forward."

He smiled and kissed the tip of her nose then led the way through the storm.

* * *

The snow was falling in earnest by the time they made it back to the lodge. A good four inches had fallen, Elise realized. Not enough to make driving impossible for Montanans used to inclement weather, but certainly enough to make it challenging.

She saw that several vehicles that had been parked out front earlier were gone. Probably families with young children, returning to their own homes for their own holiday traditions—hanging stockings, telling stories, setting out cookies for Santa.

It was Christmas. Anticipation nudged her like an old, familiar friend. Christmas, a time of hope and renewal, of miracles and second chances.

"Come home with me and spend Christmas Eve, Elise," Matt said just before they pushed open that beautiful door to Connor and Tori's home. "Will you?"

Through the windows, she could see her family inside. Both of her families. Her mother was chatting with the Castros and they all looked so happy together.

They wanted her to be happy with them, she realized. No one had been pushing her to the outside. She was the one who had refused all their efforts, the outstretched hands waiting to pull her toward them.

They would be sorry if she wasn't with them on Christmas Eve but there would be other years. This year, she wanted to be with Matt and she knew her entire crazy, complicated family would understand.

She smiled at him. "I just need to tell my mother so she doesn't worry," Elise said. She pushed open the door but before she could go inside, a huge rumbling roared above the sounds of the party coming from inside.

"What on earth?" she gasped, grabbing his shoulder.

"Avalanche," he said grimly. "Look."

Perhaps a quarter mile away down the road, she watched a vast, unrelenting sweep of snow tear away and pour down the mountain, breaking trees and moving boulders in its destructive path.

When it stopped, the only road back to town was completely covered with several feet of snow and debris.

Elise was still processing the shock of the slide as the other guests rushed out onto the wide porch.

"What the hell was that?" Connor McFarlane, still in his wedding suit, looked around. "It sounded like a hurricane."

"A slide blocked the road," Matt said. "I saw the cornice earlier and it looked unstable. I was going to warn you but got…distracted. I'm guessing all this heavy wet snow must have shifted the base enough to send the whole thing tumbling down."

"Did you see what happened? Is anybody down there?" Bo Clifton pushed his way through the crowd. "Do I need to call out search and rescue?"

"I don't think so. I didn't see anyone," Matt said. "A car had just driven through but they were a half mile down the road already when the snow came down."

"We'd better go check it out," Matt's brother Marshall said.

Several men hurried to find coats.

"By the looks of it, it's going to take several hours to dig out the road," Matt warned Connor.

"You mean we're stuck here?" someone said. "But it's Christmas Eve!"

"Oh, dear." Helen and Betty Castro exchanged distressed looks.

"I'm sorry about this." Connor immediately stepped in to take charge, as he was so good at doing. "We have plenty of food and blankets. It will be fun. We'll have a good, old-fashioned Christmas Eve."

He was being remarkably decent about sharing his wedding night with half the town, Elise thought. His words and his calm manner seemed to galvanize those remaining at the lodge into action. Immediately, people went in search of blankets and pillows and the party took on an even more festive air.

Elise was helping Haley organize an impromptu holiday classic film festival in the lodge's elaborate media room for some of the disgruntled teens when she suddenly became aware of Erin standing in the doorway, watching her with a wary expression.

"Do you guys need any help in here?"

She studied the other woman and was ashamed of herself for her small-minded jealousy of the last few weeks. None of this was Erin's fault and she had tried several times to forge a friendship. Elise had been the one pushing her away.

"Actually, I think Haley's got everything under control. I was just about to go to the kitchen and see if I can make popcorn. Want to join me?"

Erin looked surprised at the invitation but gratified.

Together, they unearthed several bags of microwave popcorn in the elaborate kitchen and stuck one in each of the pair of gleaming appliances.

They talked casually for a few moments, until Erin suddenly blurted out, "I don't want your life, you know."

Elise stared at the other woman. "I'm sorry. What?"

Erin pushed a strand of blond hair out of her face. "I know you've been struggling to deal with what happened twenty-six years ago. I just wanted to let you know I'm sorry you've been hurt by everything. I never expected... well, what happened. I'm sure you probably would have preferred if I'd never come to Thunder Canyon looking for answers."

Elise traced the events of the last month. She thought of how her life would have been different if she had never come back to Thunder Canyon. She probably never would have reconnected with this place and the people who had been so important to her once.

Through the kitchen doorway, she heard Jack Castro's gruff laugh and she thought of how kind and loving Erin's parents were and of the two brothers she had scarcely met.

And Matt.

If Erin hadn't come to Thunder Canyon to dig into the secrets of her past and discovered that fateful mistake, Elise would never have reconnected with Matt. She never would have discovered that sometimes silly girlish dreams could come true.

That secret joy shivered through her again, the love she would no longer deny, and on impulse she hugged

Erin. The other woman froze for just a moment before Erin returned her embrace.

"I've always wanted a sister," Elise said. "In a weird sort of way, it almost feels like we were twins separated at birth."

Erin laughed. "Oh, please! Not twins. Isn't our past twisted and tangled enough?"

She laughed. "Good point."

Before she could say anything else, a thin, nervous voice interrupted them.

"Excuse me, have you seen Bo?"

She turned and found Holly Pritchett Clifton, her cousin's lovely new wife.

"I think he's down assessing the avalanche with some of the other men to figure out how to dig out the road," she answered. "Is everything okay?'

"Um, not really." She gave a nervous-sounding laugh. "We're stranded here with no way into town on Christmas Eve in the middle of a blizzard."

"I know," Erin said. "Things couldn't get much crazier, right?"

Holly gave that nervous laugh. "Want to bet? I think my water just broke."

"What is taking so long?" Erica Rodriguez Traub exclaimed. "I swear, I wasn't this nervous when my own baby was born."

The entire temporary population of McFarlane Lodge seemed to be on edge, gathered in the great room while upstairs in a hastily arranged delivery room, Holly was attended by Drs. Marshall Cates and Dillon Traub—and, of course, Bo.

As the hours ticked away, everyone stranded at McFarlane Lodge hovered in a state of excitement, even the teens who emerged from the media room every once in a while to check the status of the delivery.

And then, finally, at ten minutes to midnight, a thin, high cry wailed through the house. Everyone in the great room raised up a huge cheer.

A few moments later, Marshall emerged onto the landing. He looked disheveled and tired but Elise saw the quiet satisfaction in his eyes.

"It's a boy. Mother and baby—and mayor—are all doing fine."

"Good thing we've got plenty of champagne," Grant said, breaking out another magnum.

Elise declined to drink as she kept a careful eye out the window. Down below through the snowy darkness, she could see lights moving at the avalanche site.

Once it had been determined that the threat of more snowslides had passed, Matt had hiked down the mountain through the storm for one of the Cates Construction backhoes to begin digging out the avalanche.

Elise hated thinking about him out there in the cold, but she wasn't at all surprised. That was the man she loved, strong and dependable, always willing to help out those in need.

She was still watching sometime later when she spied those lights approaching the house and a few moments later, a bundled figure walked up the porch. Soon after,

Matt walked inside and started stomping off snow in the entryway.

Her heart a sweet, heavy ache in her chest, Elise hurried to him and threw her arms around his neck, not caring at all who might be watching. She kissed him with fierce emotion and he responded with gratifying enthusiasm.

"What was that about?" he murmured after a few moments. "Not that I'm complaining."

"It's after midnight. Merry Christmas, Matt."

She helped him out of his wet gear and found hot cocoa for him. She would have thought he would want to stay right next to the fire, but he grabbed her hand and a blanket and headed out to the protected covered porch, where the gas fireplace still sent out its warmth.

He sank onto a cushioned lounger out there and pulled her onto his lap, wrapping them both in a heavy blanket until they were snug and cozy.

He kissed her deeply then, his mouth firm and demanding, and she clutched him tightly, shaken by the emotions churning through her. She longed for a little more privacy so they could make love but she knew she could be content to be with him like this, hearts and bodies entwined beneath the blanket.

The storm was lifting. Outside their safe shelter, Elise could see tiny scattered stars glimmering through the clouds.

She sighed, resting her cheek against his broad, muscled chest, his heartbeat in her ear.

"I don't want to leave," she murmured.

He gave a rough-sounding laugh. "I don't think we

can sleep out here. Even with the gas fireplace and the blankets and your considerable body heat, I'm afraid we'll freeze."

She tilted her head to study his features. "I don't mean right here, tonight, though this is pretty wonderful. I meant…I don't want to leave Thunder Canyon."

His arms tightened around her and he shifted so he could meet her gaze, his brown eyes intent and hopeful. "Are you sure? You don't like it here."

Her hair brushed his chin as she shook her head. "Not true. Part of me has always loved it here. And tonight while you were down clearing the road and we were up here waiting for Holly to have her baby, I…I can't explain it, but I was part of something. Something bigger than me, bigger than any of us."

She smiled. "It was wonderful. Really wonderful. Everyone was so concerned about each other and I realized how very much I have missed that in my life, being part of a community. I have enjoyed living in Billings but it's never felt like home. Thunder Canyon is home and it always has been. I want to stay."

His arms tightened again and he kissed her with a new intensity, his eyes filled with emotion. He had been willing to leave the town he loved for her, and his willingness to make that sacrifice meant all the more to her now, when she could see how very much her words meant to him.

"What will you do?"

"I thought I would see if Haley needs more permanent help at ROOTS. I was also thinking about opening a bookstore. Somewhere roomy and welcoming, with plump couches for people to stretch out in."

"It sounds wonderful, El." He nuzzled her neck. "I know a good builder who might be willing to give you a good deal."

"I may take you up on that."

"What about San Diego and the Castros?"

She shrugged. "Maybe I can go spend a few weeks with them once everything settles down a little."

He was quiet for a long moment. When he spoke, his tone was one of studied casualness as his fingers traced the skin at the small of her back, just below her sweater

"You know, San Diego would be a great honeymoon destination."

She stared at him, her heart pounding. "Honeymoon?"

"Maybe not next week or even next month, but that's what I want. I figured it would only be fair to warn you."

She gave a disbelieving laugh, even as her heart continued to pound. Marriage. With Matt Cates. A future with his teasing smiles and tender kisses, with that strong sense of honor and goodness. A future with him watching out for her—and then transferring that strong protective streak to any children they might have.

She pictured Holly and Bo and the tiny baby they both loved. She could easily picture a little dark-haired version of Matt chasing after them, riding in the backhoe with him, skating across Silver Stallion Lake.

A few snowflakes blew into their cozy shelter and

one landed at his temple. She kissed him there, letting the cold melt against her mouth.

"Now," she murmured. "Now everything is perfect. I love you, Matt. Merry Christmas."

And as he held her, more stars peeked out through the clouds to glitter above the quiet peace of Thunder Canyon.

* * * * *

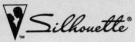

COMING NEXT MONTH

Available December 28, 2010

SPECIAL EDITION

HARLEQUIN®

A *Romance*

FOR EVERY MOOD™

Spotlight on

Classic

Quintessential, modern love stories
that are romance at its finest.

See the next page
to enjoy a sneak peek from
the Harlequin Presents® series.

*Harlequin Presents® is thrilled
to introduce the first installment of
an epic tale of passion and drama by*
**USA TODAY Bestselling Author
Penny Jordan!**

*When buttoned-up Giselle first meets
the devastatingly handsome Saul Parenti,
the heat between them is explosive....*

"LET ME GET THIS STRAIGHT. Are you actually suggesting that I would stoop to that kind of game playing?"

Saul came out from behind his desk and walked toward her. Giselle could smell his hot male scent and it was making her dizzy, igniting a low, dull, pulsing ache that was taking over her whole body.

Giselle defended her suspicions. "You don't want me here."

"No," Saul agreed, "I don't."

And then he did what he had sworn he would not do, cursing himself beneath his breath as he reached for her, pulling her fiercely into his arms and kissing her with all the pent-up fury she had aroused in him from the moment he had first seen her.

Giselle certainly *wanted* to resist him. But the hand she raised to push him away developed a will of its own and was sliding along his bare arm beneath the sleeve of his shirt, and the body that should have been arching away from him was instead melting into him.

Beneath the pressure of his kiss he could feel and taste her gasp of undeniable response to him. He wanted to devour her, take her and drive them both until they were equally satiated—even whilst the anger within him that she should make him feel that way roared and burned its resentment of his need.

She was helpless, Giselle recognized, totally unable to withstand the storm lashing at her, able only to cling to the man who was the cause of it and pray that she would survive.

Somewhere else in the building a door banged. The sound exploded into the sensual tension that had enclosed them, driving them apart. Saul's chest was rising and falling as he fought for control; Giselle's whole body was trembling.

Without a word she turned and ran.

Find out what happens when Saul and Giselle succumb to their irresistible desire in

THE RELUCTANT SURRENDER

Available January 2011 from Harlequin Presents®

MARGARET WAY

Wealthy Australian,
Secret Son

Rohan was Charlotte's shining white knight
until he disappeared—before she had
the chance to tell him she was pregnant.

But when Rohan returns years later as
a self-made millionaire, could the blond,
blue-eyed little boy and Charlotte's heart
keep him from leaving again?

Available January 2011

REQUEST YOUR FREE BOOKS!

2 FREE NOVELS PLUS 2 FREE GIFTS!

SPECIAL EDITION
Life, Love and Family!

YES! Please send me 2 FREE Silhouette® Special Edition® novels and my 2 FREE gifts (gifts are worth about $10). After receiving them, if I don't wish to receive any more books, I can return the shipping statement marked "cancel." If I don't cancel, I will receive 6 brand-new novels every month and be billed just $4.24 per book in the U.S. or $4.99 per book in Canada. That's a saving of 15% off the cover price! It's quite a bargain! Shipping and handling is just 50¢ per book.* I understand that accepting the 2 free books and gifts places me under no obligation to buy anything. I can always return a shipment and cancel at any time. Even if I never buy another book from Silhouette, the two free books and gifts are mine to keep forever.

235/335 SDN E5RG

Name _____ (PLEASE PRINT) _____

Address _____ Apt. # _____

City _____ State/Prov. _____ Zip/Postal Code _____

Signature (if under 18, a parent or guardian must sign)

Mail to the **Silhouette Reader Service:**
IN U.S.A.: P.O. Box 1867, Buffalo, NY 14240-1867
IN CANADA: P.O. Box 609, Fort Erie, Ontario L2A 5X3

Not valid for current subscribers to Silhouette Special Edition books.

Want to try two free books from another line?
Call 1-800-873-8635 or visit www.morefreebooks.com.

* Terms and prices subject to change without notice. Prices do not include applicable taxes. N.Y. residents add applicable sales tax. Canadian residents will be charged applicable provincial taxes and GST. Offer not valid in Quebec. This offer is limited to one order per household. All orders subject to approval. Credit or debit balances in a customer's account(s) may be offset by any other outstanding balance owed by or to the customer. Please allow 4 to 6 weeks for delivery. Offer available while quantities last.

Your Privacy: Silhouette is committed to protecting your privacy. Our Privacy Policy is available online at www.eHarlequin.com or upon request from the Reader Service. From time to time we make our lists of customers available to reputable third parties who may have a product or service of interest to you. If you would prefer we not share your name and address, please check here. ☐

Help us get it right—We strive for accurate, respectful and relevant communications. To clarify or modify your communication preferences, visit us at www.ReaderService.com/consumerschoice.

SSE10R

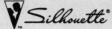

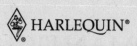

C.C. COBURN
Colorado Cowboy

American Romance's
Men of the West

It had been fifteen years since Luke O'Malley,
divorced father of three, last saw his high school
sweetheart, Megan Montgomery. Luke is shocked to
discover they have a son, Cody, a rebellious teen on his
way to juvenile detention. The last thing either of them
expected was nuptials. Will these strangers rekindle
their love or is the past too far behind them?

**Available January
wherever books are sold.**

"LOVE, HOME & HAPPINESS"

www.eHarlequin.com

har75341